ENDORSEMENTS

"Naomi Miller is a talented and wonderful author, and I can't wait to read more of her stories."

~ Molly Morris Jebber, author of
Two Suitors for Anna

"Tucked between the covers is one powerful message about forgiveness and love."

~ Shirley Chapel

"What a wonderful story of love and hope! I was hooked from the first chapter. I would highly recommend this book."

~ Toni Shiloh, author of
Risking Love

"I was pulled in to the story line from the first pages, and didn't want to put it down after I had started it. The reader who enjoys Amish fiction will certainly enjoy this one."

~ Ann Ellis

"It was a pleasure to read this book. I look forward to reading other books from this author."

~ Miss Tina's Amish Book Reviews

"I couldn't put this book down it was just that great."

~ Stacey Minter

"NAOMI MILLER HAS CRAFTED A WELL WRITTEN STORY WITH WONDERFUL CHARACTERS THAT CAPTURES THE FEELINGS OF THE AMISH COMMUNITY AND THE LONGING PERHAPS FOR SIMPLER TIMES. I WAS COMPLETELY DELIGHTED BY THIS STORY."

~ *AMAZON REVIEWER*

ABOUT *BLUEBERRY CUPCAKE MYSTERY*

"THIS IS NAOMI MILLER'S DEBUT NOVEL, AND I MUST SAY IT WAS AMAZING! I WOULD BE PERFECTLY HAPPY TO READ MORE BOOKS BY NAOMI MILLER."

~ *VINE VOICE*

"I'M READY TO PULL UP A CHAIR IN THE SWEET SHOP, SAVOR A SLICE OF CINNAMON BREAD, AND DIG INTO THIS JUICY MYSTERY."

~ *DANA MENTINK – MULTI PUBLISHED, AWARD WINNING AUTHOR*

"I WAS PULLED INTO THE STORY FROM THE VERY FIRST SENTENCE, AND COULDN'T PUT IT DOWN UNTIL I FINISHED THE LAST SENTENCE."

~ *AMAZON REVIEWER*

Ashes to Amish

A PLAIN FAIRY TALE

A PLAIN FAIRY TALE

NAOMI MILLER

RUTH MILLER

Ashes to Amish
Copyright © 2019 Naomi Miller, Ruth Miller

Ashes to Amish / Miller, Naomi. Miller, Ruth
ISBN: 978-1948733090

1. Fiction / Religion & Spirituality / Christian Books & Bibles / Christian Fiction. 2. Fiction / Romance. 3. Fiction / Christian Books & Bibles / Literature & Fiction / Amish & Mennonite.

2019940974

S&G Publishing, Knoxville, TN
www.sgpublish.com

All rights reserved. No part of this publication may be reproduced or transmitted for commercial purposes, without written permission of the publisher, except for brief quotations in printed reviews. Scripture quotations are from the Holy Bible (KJV)

This book is a work of fiction. Names, characters, places, and incidents are either products of the author's imagination or used fictitiously. Any similarity to actual people, organizations, and/or events is purely coincidental

Cover by: Expresso Designs

First Edition 2019

And we know that all things
work together for good to them
that love God, to them who are
called according to
His purpose.

~ Romans 8:28 KJV

GLOSSARY

The German/Dutch dialect spoken by the Amish is not a written language. It is solely dependent on the location and origin of each settlement. The spellings below are approximations.

Ach = Oh (exclamation)
allrecht = all right
danki = thank you
Dat = Dad
Dietsch = Pennsylvania Dutch
Englisch/Englischer = non-Amish person
freind/freinden = friend/friends
Gotte = God
Gudemariye = Good morning
gut = good
in lieb = in love
jah = yes
kaffe = coffee
kapp = head covering
kumme = come
Mamm = Mom
nee = no
Ordnung = rules for Amish life
rumschpringe = running around time for youth
verhuddelt = mixed up/confused
wunderbaar = wonderful

A NOTE FROM THE AUTHORS

Hello lovely reader,

Thank you for picking up our new novel. Hope you enjoy fairy tales as much as we do.

There are many aspects of plain living that sound like a real-life fairy tale to us. If it were possible to have a bit of technology *(it's nearly impossible to write these days without a computer)* and still live plain, we would do it in a heartbeat.

A couple of notes for you: while there are many Amish communities to chose from, we chose to create our own fictional communities close to or within well-known Amish areas so that we do not accidentally imitate any actual members of the Amish community.

Also, we have taken a bit of creative license; both in the Amish communities and in the fairy tales presented in these stories. Please understand that this is done, not out of a lack of research or respect, but strictly in the interest of the story itself.

God bless!

Prologue

The long, low, black car slowed beside the Mast's fruit stand. A single window at the back opened, and a woman's face could just be seen within the opening.

Ruth Mast watched as her young *dochder* moved over to the vehicle. She must be answering a question.

Likely some Englischer who is lost and needing directions.

Still, she smiled. Their little fruit stand

made them quite a lot of money from those *Englischers* who lost their way on the narrow and dusty back roads that were still barely a dirt trail in places.

She went back to her work, gently pulling berries from the vines that crawled all over the tall fence that ran along the edge of their smaller garden.

She had barely stripped two sections when a scream had her jerking her head up and looking toward the small fruit stand where her young *dochders* were.

She saw Aida first, running along the dirt path and wailing loud enough that her *dat* would for sure be able to hear her all the way out in the fields.

Some strange feeling had her setting down her basket and starting toward the fruit stand, and the road where the car had been stopped only moments before.

But none of her *kinner* were at the fruit stand, and no car sat parked slightly off the road by their drive. There was a cloud of dust hanging over the road, likely from where the car had pulled away quickly, throwing up dirt behind it from their turnout. She saw no one in the street or lying on the ground anywhere.

Gut. None of the kinner have been hurt.

Still, some feeling she could not explain propelled her forward. Walking past the fruit stand just as the dust began to clear from behind the long, black car, she was in time to see the all too familiar face of her youngest *dochder* as someone pulled her down and away from the back window.

A strange sound reached her ears just as her eldest *dochder* came running back from the phone shanty across the street.

"*Mamm!* Did you see the license number on that car? The police are on their way, but they asked if we saw it. Did you see it? I didn't know to look at it. I just ran for the shanty."

Ruth could feel her *dochder* gently shaking her, but she couldn't seem to make her mouth form words. All she could do was watch the spot where she had last seen her sweet little girl as the tears blurred her vision and the sobs tore at her throat.

Difficulty is a miracle in its first stage.

~ Amish Proverb

One

Ella moved through the crowded mall, wishing with each step that she had finished her wretched to-do list earlier in the day. If she had arrived an hour earlier, the crowds would not have been so packed.

She tried to push her way through the thick knot of teenagers, but quickly realized that the bag she was carrying would make it impossible to push through anything. Mentally shrugging her shoulders, she abandoned the shortest path and opted to go around the group.

Stupid premiere.

She wanted to be angry at the masses of teenagers who were crowded into the small space, but the truth of it was, she wished that she could be among them.

Well, not really among them. Her idea of what to do with a free evening was much simpler than standing in line for a movie that would probably bore her to tears.

She had wished, oh so many times, for the chance to curl up in a chair in the enormous library just down the street from this massive mall and lose herself in a book, or to sit in a coffee shop and chatter endlessly about nothing with some of the few girls in school who actually acknowledged her existence.

But it was not to be. Her cousins were the ones who got to do those things. In fact, her cousins were probably somewhere in that group of loud, pushy teens. This was precisely the sort of thing they would love to be right in the middle of.

Just then, a flash of red hair tinged with black caught her attention. When she turned to look closer, she spotted her younger cousin.

So they are here.

Ella let out a sigh at the irony. Most likely, they were both here. Which meant that they could easily have brought their shoes to drop off at the shop for repair. But their mother would never have asked them to do such a thing.

Such menial tasks were left for Ella... always Ella.

As she made her way around the group of rambunctious teens, Ella caught sight of the large neon clock above the theater entrance and she quickened her pace. If she wanted to catch the next bus, she would have to hurry.

Despite the crowded mall, she managed to make it to the shoe repair shop in minutes, but it took longer than expected to wait her turn and then to explain what was needed for each of the ten pairs of shoes that filled her bag nearly to overflowing. Ella knew she would have to practically run through the crowded mall to make it back to the front doors in time to catch her bus.

Run she did, and miraculously the crowd in front of the theater had dispersed by the time she rushed past. She only took a moment to scan the remaining crowd as she passed, but saw no signs of either cousin, so she pushed on.

She made it nearly to the doors before encountering another large group—one that stood out in a shockingly different way from the teens she'd seen earlier.

Every single one of the teens—at least they looked and acted like teens—was dressed in clothes she remembered seeing in a movie years ago for just a second or two as she handed over the popcorn her aunt and cousins had requested for their movie-watching enjoyment.

She was never invited to watch movies with them. Occasionally she managed to catch bits and pieces of a movie they rented or watched on television, but it was rare. Usually, her aunt caught her watching... breaking an unspoken rule about standing around when there was work she could be doing... and sent her back to her chores.

Her steps slowed a little as she skirted around the edges of the tight knot they formed. Their clothes might be a little funny, but they looked mostly comfortable, and everyone was wearing basically the same thing. It was not like school, where everyone found subtle ways to show up their classmates even though they were wearing uniforms. Every girl in this group was wearing dresses about the same length, and made of a similar material. The only difference she saw were the colors. The boys all wore dark pants, light shirts and suspenders with work boots or dark running shoes.

None of the girls looked to be wearing makeup. There was definitely no hair gel or other product in anyone's hair. And she saw no jewelry, though a few of them did have sunglasses tucked into the front of their shirts.

The most important thing she noticed was that they were all laughing and smiling and talking to each other. No one looked as if they were being excluded or ignored. Not one person lagged behind the group, or was obviously not a part of the group, but unable to be left behind.

The smiles were infectious... comforting... inviting... and she found herself wishing she were in the middle of this group, talking to friends she'd probably known her entire life, laughing over silly things as they strolled leisurely through the mall.

She shook her head as the group passed her, picking up her pace again as she headed for the large outer doors. And she pushed herself even faster when she saw the bus coming to a stop outside. They wouldn't stay long. She had to hurry.

If her attention had not been on the bus outside... if she had not been in such a rush... if she had chosen to move through the automatic doors instead of the manual set, she might never have crossed paths with him.

As it was, he pulled open the doors just as she pushed through, the thick glass of the door smacking into him as she rushed her way past.

"Hey!" He shouted after her, but she was running now.

"I'm sorry. I have to catch this bus. You're good, right?" She didn't wait for an answer, moving onto the bus that pulled away a few seconds later.

*　*　*

Chris looked at the door he'd just crashed into, and then into the large open entryway to the mall, where the remainder of his group lingered now.

He could see they were close enough that he could easily catch up, so he looked again at the young woman who had caused the door to smack into him. He had only caught a quick glimpse of her, but he was certain there was something familiar about her.

She stood in line to get onto the bus that had just pulled up to the curb. When she turned to say something to a person who had just gotten off the bus, he caught sight of her again.

And then he was pushing his way back through the doors he'd just come in. He could hardly believe his eyes. For sure and for certain they must be playing tricks on him, but the closer he got to the young woman, the more he could see that it was not a trick.

He was looking at the face of the only

young woman he had ever cared for! It was Aida... and she was dressed as an *Englischer*. Her hair was unbound and uncovered, swinging free for anyone to see, and she was wearing pants that were ripped in several places and a shirt that hugged her curves in such a way that he wanted to look away, even while a strong desire overwhelmed him to grab her up and take her away from all of the *Englischers* who were staring at her.

Why would she be dressed in such a way? And what is she doing here—by herself?

It made no sense. She had told him only that morning that she would not be making the trip into the city with them. She had said she had to help out in her family's road side stand over the weekend.

Why would she lie? And why would she be here of all places... dressed that way... And why did she seem as if she knew exactly where she was going... and even like she knew the people around her... as if she were here often.

While he wondered over it, he hurried toward her, moving against a crowd of people who had just gotten off the bus she was in line to board.

A few seconds later, she had stepped aboard and dropped into the seat right up front beside the window, even going to far as to look out... right at him.

He continued to push forward when he saw the hint of recognition in her expression. He waved, gestured, trying to tell her with his movements to get off the bus, but she made no move to get up. She did give him a little wave and an odd sort of half smile as the bus started to move away from the curb.

He could only stand there and watch, confused and more than a little angry.

Not only had he discovered her somewhere she ought not be, dressed as an *Englischer,* she had hit him with the door and then essentially ran away from him.

None of this makes any sense.

The thought only fueled his confusion and anger. He had no answers, and no way to find them since she was gone. He would have to wait until they were back home. And then he would have to very careful. If the wrong person overheard them speaking about this, she could be in a lot of trouble.

She had been baptized into the church last fall, accepting her place in their community after only a year of *rumschpringe.*

Is she having second thoughts? Does she not realize the consequences her actions could carry if the wrong person saw her?

He would certainly have to speak to her when he returned home. He could only hope she would be there... and appropriately dressed.

With no other options, he turned and walked back into the crowded mall, shaking his head as he went. Her behavior made no sense. It was not the behavior of the young woman he had fallen for years go.

He caught up to the others easily, since they had been moving slowly through the crowded halls.

He said nothing when he rejoined them, but Aida's younger sister must have noticed. She slowed her steps until she was walking next to him when she spoke. "You took a long time to catch up with us. Is everything all right?"

He forced himself to smile as he answered, "Everything is fine, Sarah. Someone bumped me with the door and then I got caught up in a crowd that must have just gotten off the bus outside." He shrugged, trying to make it sound as if it was no big deal.

He knew he could not let on that it was her sister who had hit him with the door and then run off, and he certainly could not tell her how Aida had been dressed.

Sarah was such a gentle young girl. She held Aida in high esteem and she would for sure be crushed by her sister's actions.

Fortunately, one of the other young girls with them called to Sarah just then, so she happily moved back to where her friend walked.

For the remainder of their trip, Chris kept a smile on his face, determined to find some way to keep everyone else from discovering what he had. He adored Aida's family, and would not want to see them hurt by something such as this.

Ach. Whatever was she thinking of?

There were no answers now. He would have to wait. But he was determined to do so as soon as possible.

Two

When she saw the horse, and the rider coming down the driveway, Aida very nearly turned and went back inside. Chris Muller was one of the few young men in the district whose company she simply did not care for in the way he seemed to feel about her.

She had tried for years—and in so many

ways—to make him aware that she did not return his feelings, but he refused to take even the most powerful hint.

Only her determination to be as Christ-like as possible kept her from being openly rude to him. *Gotte* would not want her to be rude to a fellow church member or a neighbor. She knew this to be true. Instead of hiding, she put a smile on her face and prepared to greet him as a guest.

It became apparent soon enough, that he was in no mind to extend her the same courtesy. He dismounted and stepped up to her, taking her by the elbow and leaning in to speak softly.

"Aida, we need to talk—somewhere private." His voice was cold and unfriendly, not at all what she was accustomed to from him. "It's important, Aida." He added when she continued to stand where she was.

Both his tone and his manner had Aida pushing against him, pulling her arm from his grip and moving toward the house. She didn't know what had gotten into him, but she felt *Gotte* would forgive her for being rude in this case.

He stepped in front of her though, before she could move even two steps from him. "Aida, this is serious."

She stepped back, and then to one side. There was something about his expression that had her feeling more than a bit nervous. And she did not like his demand that she go some place where she would be alone with him.

Although she tried to move away again, he would not be deterred. He stepped forward and sideways, putting himself right back in her path. "We really have to talk about this."

Finally, she found her voice. "Talk about what, Chris? You are scaring me."

"Yes, well, your behavior the other day scared me, Aida."

She shook her head and took another step back. "What behavior the other day? What are you talking about?"

"Don't play dumb, Aida. We were all there. Any one of the others could have easily seen you." The way he looked at her when he said it made her feel dirty, almost as if he were suggesting she had been somewhere and done something naughty.

She shook her head again, but he went on, his voice dropping even lower, a furious whisper now. "Do you have any idea how much trouble you would be in if Jennifer Beiler had been the one to see you instead of me? The whole district would be talking about it."

When he reached for her arm again, she pushed against him and stepped away. "I do not know what you are going on about, Christopher Muller, but I do not like the sound of it one bit."

When he started to speak, she held up a hand. "I have been nowhere but here for the past three days. And I certainly have not behaved in a way that would have the whole district talking about me."

When he stepped forward again, she rushed around him, all but running up the steps and into the house. Once inside, she kept going, not stopping until she was safely in her room.

She dropped down on the edge of her bed, her breath coming in short, hard bursts. Her heart was pounding. What could have gotten into Chris? He might not be able to take a hint about her feelings, but he had always been polite to her.

Now here he was—accusing her of something scandalous that she most certainly had not done—and being more pushy about it than she would ever have expected from him.

* * *

Outside the house, Chris stood and waited, looking up at the window he was certain belonged to Aida. Confusion and surprise had him shaking his head, and he was unsure of what to do next. He had certainly not expected her to react in such a way.

She had seen him outside the mall that day. He was certain of it. She had smiled, and waved at him with concern in her expression, as if she had know she was caught. Why was she behaving now like she had no idea what he was speaking of?

"Hey, Chris. Are you here to see Aida?" The voice of her older brother pulled his attention away from the house, and the window she was most certainly hiding behind even now.

"*Jah,* I was." He answered, but said nothing else, unsure of how much her brother would know about her behavior of late.

"Is she coming out?" When Chris said nothing, Jacob went on. "Or should I go tell her you're here?"

"*Nee,* she's not coming out. She's..." Chris

shook his head again, and then turned to face Jacob. "The truth is, I am worried for her, Jacob."

"Worried about her? Did something happen?" Jacob stepped forward then, the concern evident on his face.

Chris shook his head quickly. "Nothing has happened to Aida, Jacob. At least, not that I am aware of."

He looked back toward the house then. "But still, I am worried about her." A moment later, he turned back to look at his friend. "Have you noticed anything strange about her behavior lately?"

"Strange? Whatever do you mean? Aida does not do strange things. Chris, are you feeling well?"

Chris laughed at the expression on Jacob's face. That—and his tone—told Chris that his friend thought he must be losing his mind. "Truthfully, I am not certain anymore."

Figuring that he was not going to get an

answer about what had happened the other day, he started toward his horse. He did not want to talk about this out in the open, where anyone could hear. Even if... somehow... it was not true, Aida could get into trouble if the wrong person heard him and said something about it. Some of the youth could be terrible gossips.

Jacob set down the buckets he had been carrying toward the house and walked over to where Chris was preparing to mount.

"Wait, Chris. Let's go into the barn. We can talk there. The rest of the family is either still out in the fields or at the roadside stand."

Seeing the sense of his friend's suggestion, he nodded. He really wanted to get to the bottom of all this. Taking his horse's reins, he followed Jacob to the barn. Once they were inside, Jacob took the reins from him, leading the horse over to an area set up for visiting horses and dropped the loop in his line over a post. Then he turned back to him.

"All right. Now tell me exactly what you are talking about, Chris. What is it that has you so worried for Aida?"

Chris cleared his throat, looked around the barn, and then decided it was better if he just came out with it. "I did not want to have to tell anyone about this whole thing, Jacob. But after speaking to your sister just now, I am more worried that she may not be in full control of her senses."

When Jacob looked like he was going to interrupt, Chris rushed on. "It worries me, Jacob. Truly. She says she has no idea what I am talking about, but I saw her. I looked right at her. And she looked right at me. She hit me with a door. Then she ran away from me, and got onto a bus."

When Chris realized he was talking much too loud, he lowered his voice, but quickly went on. "When I waved, I could see that she recognized me. She knew she was caught, and now that I've confronted her with it, she says she has no idea what I am talking about."

"Now, hold on a minute." Jacob reached out and put a restraining hand on Chris's arm. "Where was this that you saw Aida, and what was so shocking about her being there?"

Chris opened his mouth to answer, but Jacob cut him off. "I mean, I presume it was some public place and not some place you should not have been as well..." He trailed off a bit, leaving his statement more a question.

"It was a very public place. It was at the mall in the city."

"Well, that's nothing to worry about." Jacob stopped. "Wait. Chris, Just wait just a minute. When did all this happen?"

"It was this past weekend, when the youth went into the city. You remember... Bishop Noah asked me to go along and help keep track of everyone. It was quite a large group who went."

When Jacob nodded, Chris went on. "Anyway, I had asked Aida if she wanted to go along. She said no... but then she—" He turned and looked away. He couldn't bear to go though it all again.

"No." At the sound of his *freind's* voice, he looked back in time to see Jacob shaking his head.

"What do you mean? It was her. I saw her —I spoke to her. Jacob, she spoke to me!"

"Chris, you could not have seen Aida in the city that day. She was here, working the roadside stand all day."

Now it was Chris's turn to shake his head. *"Jah,* that is what she told me when I asked her to go, but... Jacob, I know what your sister looks like. It was her that I saw. I am certain of it."

Jacob was still shaking his head. "But Chris, it could not have been Aida. I was there with her—all day. *Mamm* does not let any of the girls work the roadside stand alone, you know. She could not have been in the city and here as well. It must have been someone else who looked like her."

"That makes no sense, Jacob. I have been looking at Aida for five years... at every youth gathering, every Sunday service, every picnic and community event. I am telling you, this girl was Aida!"

When Jacob shook his head again, and opened his mouth to speak, Chris held up a hand to stop him. "Fine—you were with Aida, so it couldn't have been her. But Jacob, I'm telling you, she looked exactly like Aida. I mean, if it truly was not Aida, then this girl has to be Aida's twin."

Jacob reached up and took hold of Chris's arm. "Wait. What did you say?"

"I said she has to be Aida's twin. I've heard everyone has a twin somewhere, but I never really believed it." Chris shook his head a little. This conversation was not going at all the way he had thought it would. And he was beginning to worry he really might be the one losing his mind.

"Could she be? After all this time? Is it even possible?" Jacob seemed to be talking more to himself than to Chris.

"Is what possible? Could she be what?" Chris asked.

"That's it, Chris. She's Aida's twin!" Jacob whooped and turned to run out of the barn.

"What! What on earth are you talking about?" Chris called out as his *freind* headed toward his house.

Jacob suddenly stopped, then turned around and rushed back, talking the whole time, more to himself it seemed like than to Chris. "No. I can't do that. If I tell them... and it's not... no, that would not be *gut* at all... it would be very, very, very bad... it could be worse than before."

When he reached Chris again, Jacob took hold of his *freind's* arm. "I have to go there. Maybe I can find her. *Englischers* go to the mall a lot, don't they? She might *kumme* back. Then I can see for myself." He looked up at Chris, his expression filled with hope.

"You must take me."

Before Chris could answer, Jacob rushed on. "You will *kumme* with me, won't you? You saw her. You would recognize her again, *jah?* And with two of us looking, it would be much easier to spot her again, ain't so?"

Again, Chris started to answer, but Jacob rushed into another entreaty, though he didn't really seem to be asking now. "You are finished with your daily work, *jah?* You will *kumme* with me? I will go call our neighbor. He has a van. He can drive us to the city."

Chris could only nod.

Jacob rushed out of the barn again, making it several feet further from the barn before turning around and coming back in again. This time he didn't stop in front of Chris. Instead, he headed for the office, where their phone was. And while he made the call, Chris stood there, wondering what it was he had stumbled into.

His family had moved to the community five years earlier, and he had been *in lieb* with Aida Mast almost as soon as he had laid eyes on her.

He had never gotten up the nerve to tell her, but he had tried to show her in a lot of different ways. Not that it had done any good so far. She had never figured it out if one was to judge her behavior toward him.

She was always polite and welcoming, and she had ridden to several different youth gatherings with him. But she had never answered when he had shined a flashlight in her window.

As pretty a girl as she was, he figured she must have been out with some other boy from the district, and he had tried to be patient, waiting for the time to be right.

So far, it had not been.

He had fallen *in lieb* with her family as well. Her *mamm* and *dat* were *gut* folks, her brothers and sisters all wonderful. Her younger sister Sarah was especially sweet.

She treated him like a younger sister would. It was only a guess since he had no younger sisters, only three brothers, one older and two younger, but still he had always felt that way.

The Mast family had always seemed like a perfectly normal family to him. But now, with this situation, seeing someone who could only be Aida—and her insisting... and then Jacob insisting that it could not have been her. Not to mention Jacob muttering nonsensical things—mostly to himself. He was beginning to wonder if there wasn't something odd going on with the whole family.

"He is on his way." Jacob took hold of his arm again, and began to pull him outside. "*Kumme,* Chris. I will need your help."

Chris followed. If there was something odd going on with the family, he was certainly not going to send Jacob off to the city by himself. He would need someone level-headed along to help keep him from doing something foolish.

Three

Ella rushed through the crowded mall, knowing how much trouble she would be in if she did not return soon with the finished shoes.

Her cousins might not care one way or the other, but her aunt certainly would.

She tightened her grip on the heavy bag as she approached the exit doors. If she missed the bus, it would be a half hour before another arrived. The extra time would make her late—and she would have to explain the why to her aunt.

Not something she wanted to deal with, especially when she was already in such hot water for cutting it so close picking up the shoes.

Her cousins were headed to some big dance for the evening, and the car would arrive in a matter of hours to pick them up.

Outside, she headed over to the area where the bus would be stopping to pick up riders. She checked her watch and saw that she had at least five minutes before the bus was scheduled to arrive.

Putting down the heavy bag for a moment, she looked around and noticed two young men walking quickly toward the main entrance. One of them looked like the guy she had accidentally hit with the door last week.

Hoping she had enough time to apologize

for hitting him and running off, she grabbed her bag and hurried over to catch up with him and his friend.

"Hey, do you remember me? I hit you with the door last week when you were here." He stopped and turned toward her, reaching to pull his friend backwards. She kept talking, thinking of how little time she had. "I am so glad you came back, and that I saw you. I wanted to apologize then, but I was late. I would like to make it up somehow, but I have to catch my bus soon."

When he said nothing, she added, "Anyway, I'm sorry. I hope you're okay." She turned to walk away.

"Emma, wait."

"It's Ella." She stopped, wondering why he had called her Emma... she hadn't told him her name. Granted, he'd gotten it wrong, but how had he been that close? She started to walk away, but curiosity got the better of her.

"Have you been asking around about

me?" She watched them, determined to run for it if either of them made a false move.

The other boy was shaking his head. "Nee, we have not asked anyone about you, but we have been coming here looking for you every day this week, hoping to run into you again."

"You've been looking for me all week?" She nearly bolted then to get away from what sounded like trouble.

Still, there was something about the two of them that somehow made her feel that they could be trusted. She didn't know if it was their clothes or the simple way they both stood, hats dangling from their fingers, keeping a respectful distance from her. But there was definitely something.

"Why have you been looking for me?"

The boy who had been speaking took a deep breath, and then launched into what seemed to be an obviously prepared speech. "You look like my sister. And when I say that, I mean you look exactly like my sister.

You could be her twin. I mean, you really *could* be her twin."

He let out a deep breath. "I think you are, actually... her twin, I mean. I think your name is Emma... and you are my sister... and twin to my sister Aida, that is."

When he stopped talking, she looked at the boy she had hit with the door, and back to his friend, and then back to the first boy. Then she took a step backwards, and another, before the first boy stepped forward and reached out a hand toward her.

"Please, wait. I know how this must sound. I truly do. I tell you, I thought it was just as crazy as you are probably thinking it is right. Last week when I saw you, I thought you were Aida. I had no idea she even had a twin sister. Could you just give us a chance to explain better?"

After a moment, he added, "Please."

She shook her head. "I don't have any idea what either of you are talking about,

This is crazy. I don't have a sister. I don't have any brothers. How dare you? This is not funny."

When she started to turn, he moved quickly, blocking her path, so that she nearly fell against him. As she started to lose her balance, he caught her, set her back on her feet and then let go and stepped back again.

She shook her head, desperate to keep her wits about her. This had to be some sort of joke—some sick, twisted prank. There was no other explanation, unless is was a scam.

"Look, I don't have any money, and I can't get any either. I don't have anything. Nothing. Really." She insisted.

The boy spoke, his voice very gentle. "I can assure you this is not a trick of any sort. And I can promise you, we do not want anything but the truth."

Just then, the sound of the bus caught her attention.

"I've got to go." She started to turn, but both of them moved with her, blocking her path again.

"Please, Emma."

She flinched at the name. "My name is Ella."

The second boy went on. "Please, you can't go. We have to sort this out first."

And the first boy added his own pleas. "Please, just give us a chance. Can we buy you a cup of *kaffe,* or a hamburger?"

She could only nod. Somehow, there was something about these two young men that told her they were telling the truth. Whether it was actually possible or not was an entirely different matter, but she had the feeling that if she did not hear them out, they would just follow her home and continue to push the issue.

That would be bad—very bad. Her aunt would not like that one bit. She could always catch the next bus. She would be late, but it would be worth it if it kept them from following her home and causing more trouble there.

When she started to push through the mall door, the first boy was already there, holding it open for her. She muttered a thank you and walked back into the mall, amazed that everything that had been so familiar to her just twenty minutes ago, now looked almost alien.

"So, is it to be *kaffe* or a hamburger, then?"

She looked over at the first boy, who was walking right beside her now. His friend was walking behind her. She didn't want to think he was there to keep her from running away, but the thought remained.

When she opened her mouth to answer, she was just as surprised as he looked at what actually came out. "That word, does it mean what it sounds like? Does it mean coffee?" She shook her head a little. All the weirdness must be getting to her. She was sounding downright loopy.

He laughed as he answered. *"Jah...* I mean, yes. That is exactly what it means. Is that what you want then?"

She nodded. "Yeah. Coffee sounds good." She would need some caffeine if she was going to hear this story of theirs and make any sense of it. Plus, it didn't hurt that the shop was near the front of the mall. It would be easy for her to exit quickly if she needed to. "There's a great coffee shop here. It's called *Bean There.* It's pretty great."

When he nodded, she went on. "You don't have to order anything fancy. They have regular coffee, too."

"You may find it hard to believe, but I have had fancy *kaffe* before." He spoke gently as they walked through the propped open door of the coffee shop.

"Oh no. I didn't mean it like that. I just meant..." She trailed off when he laughed again. Just as they stepped up to the end of the line, he spoke again.

"I did not think you meant it any certain way. Some people take it for granted that I would not enjoy a specialty *kaffe* because I am plain. Others think it's because I am a man. I do not worry much over what others think."

He shrugged before going on. "But our youth enjoy coming to this mall. At least one Saturday every month, I find myself here. Caffeine is a *gut* way to keep my energy up."

He laughed a little. "They can be difficult to keep up with. Also, it seems a shame to miss out on *gut kaffe,* so I started ordering from *Bean There* some time ago. I have tried nearly every *kaffe* on their menu."

She smiled. The way he sounded when he talked about coffee, it sounded like he appreciated it the way she did, in a way most people did not understand at all.

Coffee was her only pleasure, the one thing she could enjoy in life, the one thing she splurged on with the meager amount of money she had access to. It was her only vice, and it kept her going when her aunt and cousins found a dozen extra little things for her to do.

And he had said he would pay. That would mean she could still have another coffee the next week. That would make her it go much better.

She only wished she had more time to actually sit and enjoy the shop, its unique decor or the wonderful music that always seemed to be playing when she came in.

He stepped up to the counter, and the young girl whose name Ella could never remember fairly lit up, her smile nearly taking over her face.

"Hey, you're back again. What are you trying today? I think there's only one or two things you haven't tried yet. What will it be?"

He motioned for Ella to order first.

The girl turned toward her, and her smile thinned out. Ella nearly giggled as she thought about what the girl must be thinking, seeing her here with a boy she clearly had a crush on.

"I'll just have my usual..." When the girl just looked at her, she went on. "A White Mocha with an extra shot."

"And for you, sir?"

"That sounds *gut*. I don't believe I have tried that one. Make that two."

"O... K... What size?"

"Venti." He answered, then looked over at Ella for confirmation. She nodded and he said it again. "Venti."

The girl nodded, took his money, and gave him his change, chirping a little *"thank you"* when he dropped the coins into their tip container, but her smile never did warm completely again.

Just then, Ella remembered the other boy. "Oh, you didn't get anything for your friend."

He was already shaking his head. "I learned that lesson the hard way. He'll get his own, and he does like plain *kaffe.*" The way he said it made it sound as if perhaps his friend had made fun of him in the past for enjoying fancy coffee.

She stepped with him to the end of the counter to wait for their coffees, watching his friend carefully as he stepped up to order. "So, you've really come here every day looking for me?"

When he nodded, but said nothing, she pressed on. "Can you maybe explain the whole thing to me a little better? I'm having a little trouble with the whole 'I look just like his sister' thing."

"*Jah,* I did too, for sure and for certain."

Just then, their coffees were called out. They moved forward to pick them up, and then he led the way to a table in the corner of the shop.

He pulled out her chair for her, and then waited to push it in for her before he took the chair across from her.

"So, you saw me last week and thought I

was his sister?"

He nodded. *"Jah,* Truly, you do look exactly like Aida. I was certain she had snuck off to the city dressed like an *Englischer* for some reason I could not imagine."

She wanted to ask what some of his words meant, but was hesitant to interrupt, so she made a mental note to ask about them later and listened as he kept explaining.

"When I got back home, I went over to speak to Aida about it. Well, she had no idea what I was talking about, so I went to talk to Jacob about it." He nodded to where his friend stood at the end of the counter, waiting for his coffee. "He told me it could not have possibly been Aida that I saw because he was there at home with her all day."

His friend, appeared next to their table then and pulled out the chair next to his friend, his chair scraping a little as he dropped into it. "Ah, you are explaining." When the first boy, whose name she still didn't know, nodded, Jacob said. *"Gut."* and started to drink his coffee.

"Anyway, the mention of how much you look like Aida got Jacob's attention, and he asked me if I would *kumme* back to the mall with him to see if we could find you." Jacob nodded, but the first boy went on explaining.

"And we have. We came every day this week at about the same time I saw you that first time, because we did not want to miss you."

"But that does not explain how I look like your sister or why you thought my name was Emma." She directed this to Jacob.

"Ah, that. Well, that answer is easy. I believe you are my sister, and twin to Aida. You, Emma, were kidnapped when you were just three years old."

Four

Ella walked slowly up the brick path was as familiar to her as the house it led to. This was all she knew, all she could remember, the only place she had ever called home.

But if what these two boys told her was true, it was not her home, and it never had been. She belonged somewhere else, to parents she could not remember, with a family she didn't know.

And a twin sister I've never met...

The thought terrified her. How was it possible that she had no memories of a family she had known for three years of her life?

Could it all just be a mistake?

That was another horrifying thought. What if they were wrong? What if it were just a passing resemblance? What if she came home, told her aunt what they'd said... and they were wrong. What would Aunt Silvia say... what would she do? How would she react to the news that her sister had apparently kidnapped Ella when she was a baby?

Would she be relieved, not to be responsible for another mouth to feed, something she mentioned almost daily, or would she be angry to lose the last link she had to her beloved sister?

There was no way of knowing. All Emma

could do was walk up to the door and introduce Jacob and Chris to her aunt, explain all that they'd told her, and hope for the best.

She didn't bother to knock, unlocking and then pushing open the heavy door, quickly moving inside, waiting until both boys were in the foyer before turning to close it again.

Chris put a hand just below hers on the door and helped her to push. She fought against the blush that tried to fill her cheeks with a tell-tale pink. There was no reason to be embarrassed about needing help with the heavy door. Though, deep down, she knew that wasn't really what had a heat rushing to her cheeks.

She didn't want to think about what it was that made her feel as if her heart might beat right out of her chest any moment. Fortunately, she didn't have to.

"Ella, where have you been? We are going to be late!" Her cousin's voice momentarily distracted her from the worry, the embarrassment, and brought with it an entirely new set of nerves.

She had been sent to the mall with a very specific task to accomplish. Her cousins would not care that she had absolutely no control over the crazy news she would likely have to share with her cousins as well as her aunt.

Desperate to find some way to get them out of the house before she spoke to her aunt, she turned to face her cousin and held up the bag she'd carried in. "I'm here now, and I have your shoes." She hurried along beside her cousin, turning back a moment later, remembering almost too late, the two young men who had come in with her.

"I'll be right back. If you wouldn't mind waiting in the front parlor…" She trailed off as she gestured helplessly to the room beside them.

Both men nodded and walked into the room. Ella cringed as they disappeared, thinking of the decor that would be perfectly normal to most, but likely shocking to two young men who lived what she felt certain would be an ultra conservative lifestyle.

With a shrug, she rushed to catch up with her cousin. There was nothing to be done about it. They had been gracious about everything so far. Hopefully, they would go on the way they'd begun.

"What is taking you so long, Ella!" Victoria's demanding voice distracted her again, and she rushed to apologize, but was cut off.

"Oh, never mind. Just give me those." She took the bag from Ella's hand and headed off toward her room.

Ella took several deep breaths and turned toward the front of the house again... only to be brought up short by the sight of her aunt, standing barely a foot away. Her stiff posture nearly made up for her lack of height.

Even though she were only an inch or two

taller than Ella when she was wearing the ridiculous heels she insisted made her look dignified, that ramrod straight posture coupled with an overbearing personality had always made her aunt seem frightfully tall and imposing.

"And just where have you been? Dallying again?" Ella cringed at the acid in her aunt's voice.

She would have to be in a foul mood already.

The thought was no comfort. She told herself her aunt would have been in a foul mood anyway in a few minutes.

"Aunt Silvia, I have something I need to tell you." She spoke quietly, determined to do everything possible to keep from setting off the temper that had netted her more than one slap.

Ella's aunt just stood there, saying nothing. It was impossible to tell if she were more angry than she had already been or not.

However, a moment later, when Ella did not go on, the frown deepened and it was all Ella could do not to cringe in anticipation.

"Well, girl... what is it?" She gave Ella exactly one second to speak, barely time to open her mouth, before she went on. "Out with it!"

"There is really no need to be angry with Emma. Her tardiness is entirely our doing." Ella gasped when Jacob spoke up from behind her aunt. If he had known her aunt the way Ella did, he would have known trouble was coming.

She turned slowly, taking in everything about Jacob as she did. Ella could practically hear the disappointment spreading over her face.

"And you are..."

It was all Ella could do not to gasp again. Her aunt's response was not at all what she'd been expecting.

She must have been caught off guard by

his appearance.

It was the only thing Ella could think of that made even the slightest bit of sense.

Jacob walked forward, a hand outstretched toward her aunt. "My name is Jacob Mast, and I have *kumme* here to find Emma..." After a beat, he added, "my sister."

Ella could have sworn she saw her aunt flinch—and she could not help but wonder if she were flinching at Jacob's bold maneuver or his direct delivery, but she gave no outward signals or signs, only a straighter back, if that were even possible.

Time stretched out painfully as the four of them stood there in silence, each waiting for the other to speak. Aunt Silvia stared hard at the two young men standing in front of her and Ella found herself wishing her aunt would just say something to break the silence. Someone would have to speak, eventually, but Ella was determined it would not be her.

The way Jacob had come out with essentially everything Ella had intended to work up to slowly was likely the reason for her aunt's silence.

Aunt Silvia rarely spoke unless she had already calculated every single work that would come from her and everyone around her, and of course, that was simply not possible in this situation.

Finally, unexpectedly, it was Chris who broke the silence.

"Mrs. Wharton..." He began gently, but Aunt Silvia cut him off sharply.

"I am Mrs. Stockton. Wharton was my sister's name."

"Very well, then. Mrs. Stockton, we came here as a courtesy, to discuss the matter with you." Again, Aunt Silvia cut him off.

"You think you've only to fill Ella's head with this nonsense, and she will go off with you." With a "humph" she turned to face her niece.

Ella cringed as her aunt's hard stare

fairly bore into her.

"I know you are smarter than this, Ella. Surely you haven't been giving the nonsense these two are feeding you any real weight." It was not a question.

Ella knew she was expected to agree immediately, not argue, no matter how much she wanted to. Without another thought, she found herself nodding.

"As I expected." With a nod, Aunt Silvia turned smartly back to face the boys. "Now then. You will remove yourselves from this house immediately or I will have you removed."

Ella watched as a muscle in Chris's jaw twitched, but he, like Jacob, turned and walked back to the front door.

However, before they crossed the threshold, Jacob turned back to look directly at Aunt Silvia. "This is not over. One way or another, I mean to have my sister back. *Gotte* is on our side."

After a moment, he went on. "I thing you

will find that the brightest lightning *kummes* from the darkest clouds, and the purest faith from the most severe trials."

"Is that meant to be a threat?" Aunt Silvia's voice was positively frosty by now.

He shook his head, his expression one of pity, as though she were the one too slow to understand something as simple as breathing. "Tis a well-known proverb my people hold dear. We will be in touch." And then, before she could say anything else, they were gone.

Ella tried to back up, to slip away before her aunt could turn and unleash her anger on her, but she'd gotten no more than a foot before her aunt turned

"And just what were you thinking, bringing them here, to our home?" She turned, paced away from Ella, but she knew her opportunity to slip away had gone. All she could do was to stand there and take whatever her aunt decided to unleash on her.

"Do you have any idea how stupid your behavior was today? Bringing them here, letting them inside. What am I to do with you, Ella!" She nearly exploded as Emma shrank away from her. "Now they know exactly where we live. They'll be back, all right." A moment later, she added, "Go to your room. I will deal with you later."

The words were spoken in her aunt's usual hard voice, but with an edge of something Ella did not quite recognize.

At the moment, she really didn't want to think about what it could be. Whatever was going on with her aunt, she would certainly bear the brunt of it.

* * *

Outside the house, Jacob and Chris returned to the van driven by their *Englischer* neighbor, their steps slow, hesitant, heavy.

"You know, I had a feeling this would not

be easy." Jacob spoke slowly, quietly. "Somehow I allowed myself to think that it might all work out quickly and easily when Emma was so quick to believe us and bring us to her house."

Chris nodded, but said nothing. He had been hopeful, but he'd not expected things to go smoothly or easily.

"I am not ready to give up though."

"Of course not." Chris insisted. He might not have hope to offer his friend, but he would offer all the support he could muster. When Jacob had explained the whole situation, Chris had thought of what it would be like to lose one of his brothers, and the feeling was one he would not wish on anyone.

"I wonder if we should keep this between us for now." He said it like he was not expecting Chris to answer, but also like he was looking for an opinion, so Chris gave his.

"I think that would be a *gut* idea... at

least until you have a better idea of what you want to do next." There was no point in upsetting the family when things were such a mess as they were right now. For sure it would only make things more difficult for them all.

They got into the van and told Jack they would like to return home. To his credit, he made no comments about Emma not coming with them, even though he must have heard them talking about who she was on the way to her house.

As he drove, Chris thought about the situation and how the Mast family could get their lost daughter back. It would not be easy. No *Englischer* gave up so easily as the plain folk did when they were pushed... or in the wrong about something.

Although, in this case, there were so many things that made no sense. By her own account, the woman Emma had grown up thinking of as her mother was gone, and had been for years. And her aunt and cousins showed her some very strange treatment, indeed.

Why, the way the cousin had acted when Emma walked in with her heavy load, it was almost as if she were a servant instead of a member of the family.

If that is the case, could that be why they were so reluctant to let her go?

It was a frightening thought, but nothing else made sense... no matter how he puzzled it all out.

"Do you... I mean, did you notice..." Jacob trailed off, after halting mid-question twice, so Chris pressed a little.

"Jah, did I notice what?"

"It's probably nothing... I mean, I'm probably wrong, but did it seem to you like they think of Emma more like a servant than a member of the family?" His voice was very hesitant, almost as if he were actually asking Chris to tell him he was wrong.

But Chris was not at all certain he was

wrong. "I did notice that. I was just thinking about it. Do you think that could be the reason they do not want to let her go... they don't want to pay for a servant when they have one who works for free?" She certainly had not given him the impression that they paid her anything for all of the work she did.

Jacob shook his head a little before answering. "I don't know. I want to say it sounds too strange to be true, but..." He shook his head again as he trailed off.

They sat in silence for a long time as the van traveled from fancy neighborhoods, back to the city, then to the interstate, and finally to the smaller, narrower simple roads of their familiar community.

When they pulled into Jacob's yard, he repeated his earlier question. "So, we should keep this between us for now, *jah?*"

Chris nodded. "*Jah,* I think that would be the easiest on everyone. We cannot tell your family that you found Emma—and then tell them we could not even bring her here for them to see."

Jacob was nodding, long before Chris finished. "You are absolutely right. It would break poor *Mamm's* heart to know her daughter is out there somewhere, but she cannot see her."

What neither of them noticed was Aida standing just inside the barn, hidden by the shadows, but close enough to hear their conversation.

Five

For weeks, Ella fretted. While it was somewhat nice, not having to run errands constantly for her aunt and cousins, she was more than a little tired of being stuck in the house.

She had made plans for the summer. With school out and her cousins off on vacation with their friends, she had expected to have a little bit of time to herself. But it was not to be. Her aunt had insisted she could not be trusted and forbade her to leave the house alone.

She had read every single book she owned for about the hundredth time, and dared not ask for more. She had no television to watch, and with no cousins at home, there was absolutely no one to talk to.

Her aunt spent most of her days either in her office with the family lawyer, or in the parlor watching the front door—not that Ella would have tried to sneak out with her in the house, and certainly not with her aunt's driver always hanging around outside.

If only Aunt Silvia would go out, and hopefully take her driver with her, I could leave. I would simply walk out the front door and... well, I would do something... go somewhere.

If only she would leave...

About the only thing Ella could do to pass the time was clean. So that was what she did with her time. She cleaned every room in the house thoroughly, top to bottom, leaving no piece of furniture unmoved and no hidden area untouched.

She cleaned and scrubbed and polished and dusted and shined everything she could get her hands on.

When she'd been through the entire house, she went back to her books, but after a month of being housebound, she was nearly ready to try and sneak out. She felt as if she were slowly going insane. Her aunt had forbidden her to leave, but she rarely spoke to her, and she never, ever wanted Ella to be in the same room with her.

Finally, one afternoon when her aunt left the house to go to a meeting of one of her social clubs, Ella gathered up the nerve to leave. As long as she returned before her aunt, there shouldn't be a problem.

It was no surprise when she ended up at

the mall at her favorite coffee place, using change she had collected between seat cushions and found on her cousins' floor to pay for her drink.

It was a complete surprise, when she turned around to find a seat, to discover a familiar face. He was sitting at one of the tiny tables, and when she spotted him, she was certain he had been preparing to leave.

When he looked her way, she smiled and waved at him. Instead of waving back, he looked away, an unreadable expression on his face, his eyes fixed not on hers, but on someone else.

Ella looked to her left, where he was looking so intensely, fully expecting to see the young man who insisted he was her brother, but there was a young woman sitting across from him at another table.

A gasp caught in her throat.

She rarely took much time to look at her face in a mirror, especially since her appearance didn't seem to matter to her aunt or cousins. However, she had seen her reflection enough times over the previous seventeen years to know when she was looking at it.

And right now she was looking at her own reflection, albeit the young woman before her was wearing a stiff white *kapp* over her tightly bound hair, and a long dress of a deep blue material, but there was no question that their faces were identical, right down to the slight crookedness of their left ear.

"Are you all right, Emma?" The voice beside her startled her less than the face in front of her. Chris must have finally made his way over to her.

She could only shake her head in response. There was nothing about this situation that made her all right. Aunt Silvia might be able to argue with the two boys, but there was no way she could argue with the girl who was clearly... obviously her sister, her mirror image, her... twin.

She gasped again at the thought—and all that went along with it.

She had a twin sister, and a family—one she'd been kept from all these years, people she belonged with, but had no memories of, a mother and a father... who might actually want her around.

What am I going to do now?

But she had no answer. She had no clue about how to move forward; no idea of what she should do now.

She stood there, looking at the face in front of her, the one that was identical to her own, though when she looked closer, she could see that there was a tiny difference in the shape of their lips and a darker tint to the young woman's skin.

From what Ella had been able to find out in the research she'd done at the library— after the first time she had seen their group at the mall—she knew the Amish people tended to spend a great deal of time outside, working the land. So the darker skin made sense... and she was pretty certain no Amish person would ever get a spray tan. The thought of it made her want to giggle.

Also, there was a softness to the features that Ella knew was missing from her own. Aside from losing her sister at a very young age, there was nothing about the face she was looking at that showed signs of hardship. She might work hard, but none of it weighed on her.

But then, she also has family to help with everything.

Ella pushed aside the bitterness. There was nothing she could do to change her circumstances. But maybe there was something she could do now. Here was proof, staring her in the face, that she belonged to another family. She would be silly to ignore it.

Just as she opened her mouth to say something, she wasn't entirely sure what, but something, there was a gentle pressure on her arm. When she turned, Chris was there, holding the coffee she'd ordered and forgotten about completely.

"They called your name. I figured you didn't hear." He smiled gently as he held out the cup to her.

"Thanks. Yeah." She took the cup, wrapped her hands around it, tried to figure out what she wanted to say to these people who were more family to her than the only family she'd ever known—and somehow still complete strangers.

"Do you want to join us?" Chris asked. All she could do was nod... again.

He was already pulling the chair he had been sitting in around the table, closer to her. When she sat down, he pulled the remaining chair over to where he had been sitting a few minutes ago.

"So, you go by Ella?"

She looked over at the young girl asking the question and nodded.

"I am Aida." Her voice was unexpectedly

quiet—so unlike her own. It was the first noticeable thing that they did not share.

How many times had her aunt lectured her over the years about speaking too loudly, too forcefully, to strongly?

Too many to count.

And, no sooner had the thought come than Ella reminded herself that Silvia was not really her aunt.

Does she know?

Panic took hold of her as the thought began to sink in. Her mother... No, not her mother. A stranger had taken her from her true family and lied to her. Then she had died and left Ella behind with people who were not her family—and never really had been.

People who did not want her around at all. Which must be why they were only too happy to have her clean up after them. They knew she wasn't really family.

They know. They must know.

Her own sister could not have hidden a

thing like that.

Suddenly, she was very angry. And the anger would have consumed her, but the next question distracted her.

"And as an *Englischer*, you're still going to school?"

Ella nodded again, almost absently as she sipped her coffee and toyed with a loose thread on her faded jeans. Then she thought about the question a bit more and realized she hadn't answered entirely truthfully. "I mean, no. I'm not going to school right now. We're out for the summer." A moment later she added, "Do you go to school in summer?"

Aida smiled and shook her head a little. "No. We do not attend school during the summer months, either. We also do not attend school beyond the eighth grade."

Ella thought about that for a minute. There was nothing about the young woman's speech or manners that gave the idea that she was poorly educated. And both

Chris and Jacob had given her the impression that they were intelligent, well-educated young men. It was difficult for her to believe all of that came from only an eighth grade education.

They must have really good schools.

Before she could say so, Aida spoke up again.

"Do you have a job? Or a boyfriend?"

Ella frowned when Aida asked about a job, but laughter bubbled out of her at the thought of having a boyfriend. The very idea was ridiculous.

As if Aunt Silvia would allow such a thing.

Just as she reminded herself again that Silvia was not really her aunt, the young woman spoke again. "I'm sorry. Which part of my question was funny?"

Ella waved a hand as she answered. "Oh, it's so many things really."

"*Allrecht.*" There was more than confusion in her voice, but Ella continued her explanation, hoping she could explain it all right.

"I was just thinking how ridiculous an idea it was. Even if any of the boys at school paid a bit of attention to me—which they don't." She laughed, but went on quickly. "Anyway, Aunt Silvia would be horrified at the very idea of my dating."

She put up a hand again to stop the question she could see forming on the lips that were identical to hers—even down to the color.

"I know. She's not really my aunt. That's the other bit that's so funny. All these years I have bent until it felt like I would surely break, trying to do what she wanted but never actually succeeding." She waved a hand then to the two people sharing the table. "And now I find out that she was never related to me at all."

She laughed again, but rushed on before either of them could interrupt. "I cannot tell you how liberating a feeling it is, to know that I might actually have a different life out there somewhere—another choice."

Aida was nodding, a look of confusion and concern on her face. Chris, who had met Silvia, and was likely not one bit surprised at Ella's confession, looked suspiciously like he wanted to laugh... or smile, at the very least.

Ella took another sip of her coffee.

"So, no job either, then?" Aida asked after a few moments.

Ella shook her head again. "There's far too much at home that needs doing, and I am the one it all seems to fall to." She shrugged.

The hurt had long ago faded. She had figured out almost immediately that Silvia did not relish having the unexpected responsibility thrust upon her. However, it was beginning to make a lot more sense to her now.

Having a grieving niece added to your household would be difficult, but having a child you know to be no blood relation to you suddenly become a member of your household was something else.

For a moment, Ella wondered why Silvia had gone through with it. Surely she would have known she could easily have sent Ella off to an orphanage. There likely would not even have been any questions, given the circumstances.

But Ella knew why she'd gone through with the sham. Not only would it would have sullied her sister's reputation if anyone had learned the truth. It would also have threatened her position in the strange little high society that Silvia had been trying to push her way into for years; the society that her sister had been very much a part of.

So, she had taken in the orphan—who really wasn't an orphan, and had made her place clear to everyone, sprinkling in a heavy dose of guilt along with the tiny little attic room and the pittance of an allowance she was careful to dole out each month, no matter what.

Ella could not help but wonder about that. Realizing that Silvia was not indeed her aunt raised as many questions as it answered... maybe even more.

"I am wondering if you would want to *kumme* home with us, to meet the rest of the family."

Ella started to refuse, to make an excuse, as was her habit from many years of doing just that. But she stopped to think about what she really wanted to do in this situation.

It was not as if she were doing anything wrong. She was going to meet her family, her real family—and Silvia really had no way to stop her. Especially since she wouldn't even know Ella had left the house unless she arrived home from her meeting before Ella returned.

"Yes, I would like that very much. Can we go now?" She stood, feeling rushed now that she had made the decision, feeling somewhat certain that Silvia would somehow appear and stop her.

Chris and Aida looked at each other, but stood with her, both stepping to the side as they pushed in their chairs and gathered up the trash on their small table. If her behavior was strange, neither of them said anything.

Maybe they're afraid they'll scare me off if they say something.

As they walked toward the front entrance, Ella realized that she was looking all around her and over her shoulder for the familiar figure of her aunt.

She took a deep breath and forced herself to relax. Then she told herself there was no wrong in going to meet the people who were her actual family—and nothing Silvia could do to stop her from doing so.

Still, there was an odd sensation at the back of her neck as they walked the wide hallway, heading for the front doors of the mall.

When they stopped just outside the doors, she looked down at the ground, fidgeted with the hem of her shirt, sipped her coffee, took deep breaths—anything to distract herself from the sudden desire to run and run, far away from everything.

At the sound of an engine, she looked up, letting out her breath in a sudden explosion of air when she saw it was not Silvia's town car.

She didn't know what she'd expected, but it wasn't the large white van that had stopped right beside where Chris was now helping Aida in. Ella hadn't even asked them how they would be getting to their home, but she'd been fairly certain it would be by buggy... not a big van.

Six

Their trip to the country was as uneventful as Ella could have hoped for, unless you counted the questions that Aida peppered her with the entire way.

From the time they'd pulled out of the mall parking lot, she had begun asking questions, waiting only long enough for Ella to answer before asking another.

She'd asked about school, about Ella's friends—of which there really were none to speak of. She'd asked about the house Ella had grown up in, and about the mother she barely remembered.

Ella was certain there was more Aida had wanted to ask about the woman who had absconded with her twin sister, but Aida was either uncomfortable with the subject or she thought Ella would be, because she skirted the issue carefully.

She asked what Ella meant when she'd said everything at home somehow fell to her to take care of—to which Ella answered as diplomatically as possible, moving the conversation along as quickly as she could. Even knowing that Silvia was not really her aunt, she felt strange about speaking ill of her. She had allowed her to stay in her home—the only home she remembered, instead of sending her to an orphanage.

Her life there might not be wonderful, but Ella was certain life in an orphanage would most likely be worse. At home all she was asked to do was clean up and take care of Silvia and her daughters. In an orphanage, her size and penchant for reading would likely have made her a target.

It was a fear she had nursed for years. After her mother... no, not her mother... had died, Ella had waited for Silvia to decide she was too much trouble, certain one wrong move would be all that was needed for her to send Ella off to an orphanage. It was one reason she had worked so hard in the beginning. She had not wanted to give anyone a reason to think she was not deserving of her place in the only home she had ever known.

She said none of this to Aida. She did not even want to know what this young woman would think of her thoughts and worries... much less what her life had been like over the past ten years.

What would she think of me?

For some inexplicable reason, Ella was suddenly very worried over what Aida thought of her... or what she would think of her life.

For the rest of the drive she paid close attention to each question, doing her best to answer each one as simply as possible while still being truthful.

It was not an easy thing.

It was sometime later when Ella noticed a difference in both Aida and Chris. There was something more relaxed about their behavior all of a sudden.

And then they were pulling off the road and turning down a gravel driveway. Aida stopped asking questions and Chris placed a gentle hand on Ella's shoulder, rested it there for several long seconds, gently squeezed, and then let it drop.

She looked back at him, certain the sudden fear that had risen up unexpectedly in her was written all over her face.

What would these people think of her?

Was there still a chance this whole thing was just a mistake? What if they did not want anything to do with her, being from what they called the *Englischer* world? What would she do then?

She didn't voice a single question. She didn't dare. She didn't really want to know the answers. She just watched as they traveled slowly along the gravel drive.

The land around them was green as far as she could see. On one side of the drive, there were rows and rows of what she presumed to be corn. On the other, there seemed to be all sorts of things growing. She easily spied the rows of tomatoes in various shades of red, yellow and green.

They crested a small hill and she caught sight of a house. It was large, neat, and welcoming. The house itself was a basic white, but the wide flower boxes that marched along the front of the house were a cheerful yellow and the roof was a deep, beautiful blue. The front door, shutters, and trim was painted to match the roof, though a darker shade of blue.

As the van made a wide circle around the large open area in front of the house, she could see a large barn and several other buildings grouped together to one side of it. Each one was painted the same white as the house, with the same bold blue tin roofing. They were neat, clean and as they pulled up, several young people came outside.

The van finally came to a stop in front of the house, and Jacob was already striding across the driveway from the direction of the barn. He opened the door with a cautious expression that changed when he saw her sitting in the middle seat next to Aida.

Getting from the van to the house was a bit of a blur to Ella later. When she thought about it, all she could remember was a crowd of teens and kids all around her, asking questions at once, while herding her toward the house.

For some reason Chris had not come into the house with them, and she had to struggle to keep her feet going in the same direction as the others.

She felt as if he were here, she might have some feeling of detachment from all of the people around her whom she really did not know at all.

After all, he had no stake in all of this. He had only been helping out a friend. He wasn't related to her. He had no reasons to want her here. He had no strong feelings about her as far as she could tell. If he had stayed, she might have felt a bit less pressured, but she told herself there was no guarantee of that.

Besides, the group of people around her really gave her no choice but to follow this whole thing to its conclusion.

So, she allowed them to sweep her along out of the van, across the driveway, up the stairs, and into the house.

And the first person they saw once they

all came through the front door must have been their mother... her mother... her real mother.

There were a dozen emotions rushing through Ella as she looked at the small woman in front of her. This was the woman who had given her life, the woman who had taken care of her for the first few years of her life, the woman she had been stolen from, the woman who had cried over her, perhaps mourned her.

She was a slight woman with deep blue eyes and graying blond hair tucked up under her *kapp*. There were lines around her mouth and eyes, which Ella hoped were a sign that she smiled often. She wore the same simple dress her other daughters wore, in a darker shade of green than Aida's, but not quite black. Her feet were bare.

She looked like she had been walking toward the front door, likely to find out what all the commotion was about, but when she looked up and caught sight of Ella, she stopped moving forward. Not a moment later Jacob rushed forward with one of the other boys to catch her as she started to sway.

Aida kept a tight hold of Ella's hand, but all of the other girls in the group moved forward to help as well. The lot of them helped their mother into a chair in the front room before turning back to wait for Aida to guide Ella into the room as well.

"Emma?"

Ella tried not to flinch at the name. She should have known they would call her that since it had clearly been her name at one point, but hearing it was something entirely different. She might have been named that at birth, but she had been Ella for nearly fourteen years of her life. She was used to the name, comfortable with it. It felt more like her after all this time, and she wasn't sure if she should insist on being called Ella or just give in and let them call her whatever they wanted.

Fortunately, Aida spoke up then. "She goes by Ella, *Mamm.*"

"Ella?" The soft voice barely carried to where Ella and Aida had paused in the doorway of the large room, but Aida was nodding beside her even as she started to speak up and tell the woman she could call her anything she liked.

This woman was her mother, her real mother, her flesh and blood, the woman who had lost her all those years ago. *Who am I to tell her she has to call me by the name given to me by the woman who stole me from her?*

But she was nodding. "Ella then." She held out her hands and Aida moved forward slowly, pulling Ella along with her.

Ella went willingly, though she did stumble a little as her vision blurred with the unexpected tears that welled up in her eyes with no warning.

As she moved forward, the gravity of the

situation began to really sink in, slowing her even further and the weight of all she had endured over the last ten years had her dropping to her knees in front of the chair where her mother sat.

By the time she had collapsed on the floor in front of her mother, the tears were flowing freely. She leaned forward instinctively and buried her face in the apron that filled her mother's lap.

Warm arms came around her and then she was enveloped in warmth as the others joined their mother. She had no way of knowing which arms belonged to whom, but there was a strong feeling of belonging that she had never known before.

Here, in the most unexpected place, and surrounded by the most unexpected family, she was finally home.

Seven

less emotional, mostly since her sisters
were still in attendance. They all seemed
quite reluctant to go back to whatever they
had been doing before she arrived, moving
along with her from room to room in an
informal sort of tour of the house that her
mother led before her father came in from

the fields.

When he did come in, he folded her into a hug, letting go only to pull Aida into the embrace with her a moment later. She could hear sniffles from somewhere behind her and then his hold loosened a bit as their mother slipped in under his arm on her other side.

How long they stood like that she could not have said, but when they did finally move apart, she was surprised to see that they were alone at last.

She discovered a few minutes later that the women of the family had moved to the kitchen while the boys had gone outside to finish up the jobs they'd left undone in order to come and meet her.

It was no surprise that dinner turned out to be a noisy and slightly messy affair, in a house with eight siblings, including herself, plus the husband and two small children she was surprised to find went with her oldest sister, and a young woman joining them whom Jacob was evidently courting.

She was surprised at how easily they all included her, not only in the conversation, but in family jokes and stories. Everyone seemed to have at least one story to tell her about someone or other and multiple family members would add comments to each story as it was being told.

During all of this, food was passed from person to person in large bowls and on wide platters. When she took too little, the next person would only scoop up more and pile it on her plate before taking their own portion.

At one point she had to hold up a hand to stop Aida. "Wait, please. I will never be able to eat this much and I don't want to waste the food."

Aida looked to their mother, her mouth slightly open in surprise. Ella looked over to her as well. She didn't think what she'd said was really that shocking, but maybe she'd somehow insulted someone.

"Please forgive your sister, Ella. It's just that you're so thin. I'm certain she just wants to be certain you have all you want."

"Jah. Exactly." When Ella looked back to Aida beside her, she went on. "I just thought you were worried you might be taking too much. I want you to eat what you want. That's all."

Ella nodded. "And I will, I promise. I just know how much I can eat and this is more than that already."

The next comment came from Jacob. "So, you're on one of those diets that are so popular with the *Englischers,* then?"

Ella laughed then. The very idea was ridiculous. She had never had access to enough food to possibly get fat enough to need a diet. And if she had, her constant running would work any excess off in a hurry.

"No. It's nothing like that, I promise." She stopped herself before saying more, not wanting to explain everything about her treatment at the hands of people she had been certain for more than a decade were family.

For several seconds, an uncomfortable silence fell over the group. Fortunately, their mother spoke up, commenting about the circumstances that had led them to finding Ella.

"So, Aida, I suppose this explains your sudden interest in the city." She smiled at both Ella and Aida beside her.

Not a moment later, their father added, "I admit you have me a bit worried. I thought you might have found an *Englischer* boy you were interested in."

Ella was not quite sure how to interpret the sound of choking from beside her. She turned to look at Aida, and was relieved to see that her sister was laughing, not choking.

She didn't ask the question that was burning in her mind, though she really wanted to, about why their behavior made it sound as if that would be a bad thing. She had already brought the conversation to a halt and had no wish to again.

One thing was certain, she had a lot to learn about her new family.

*   *   *

After dinner, their mother and one of the older girls cleared the table and headed into the kitchen to start cleaning up. Ella picked up her plate and started to follow, but Aida took it out of her hands and breezed past her with a smile.

She sat there for several long seconds, uncertain of what to do. There was never a meal she didn't clean up after. Should she follow and insist on helping or should she ask someone to give her a ride back to the city?

Are they expecting me to spend the night? Are they expecting me to stay forever? What would I do here?

There was no panic, so far, but there was a great deal of confusion.

Yes, the woman she'd always thought of as a mother had clearly taken her from her family, but Ella had no idea how to proceed. Would staying here get her new family in trouble... or get her into trouble? Would they count her as a runaway if Silvia called the police because she never came home?

A small hand dropped onto her shoulder just as her mother spoke from behind her. "I can see you are worrying. What is it, *lieb?*"

She answered as honestly as she could, her words spilling out in a jumble. "I just don't know what to do. I mean, do I stay or do I go back to the city tonight? And if I stay, is that going to cause problems? I don't want anyone to get into trouble over this, not me, and certainly not you." When her mother said nothing, she rushed on. "Do you even want me to stay?" At that, her mother wrapped her arms around Ella and held tight.

"Oh, my sweet girl. Of course we want you to stay."

Ella let out the breath she hadn't realized she was holding as her mother went on. "We never want to let you go again, not for anything." She squeezed a little tighter for a moment before letting go a little and leaning back to look at Ella. "But you are right. You will have to go back sometime, and we will likely have to deal with the law some time to settle all of this." She pulled Ella close again and just held.

After several long moments, she spoke again, her voice quiet. "But maybe not tonight." She leaned back again. "Tonight, we can just be a family, *jah?*"

Ella could only nod. Being a family sounded really good to her.

She never did get a chance to help with the cleanup. Instead, she was pulled into the living room, where she told her mother all about her life, careful to gloss over the worst of it, and answer most of the same questions Aida had asked on their ride out that afternoon.

Her mother sat in an ancient rocking chair by the fireplace, her fingers busy with some sort of mending while she talked and listened. She paid little attention to her fingers though. Obviously, whatever it was, she did the work so often her fingers knew just what to do all on their own.

Her father sat in a chair across from them for a time, listening, asking a few questions, but mostly shaving bits of wood from a block he held in his hands, turning this way and that—and paying as little attention to what his fingers were doing as her mother was.

At some sign she'd clearly missed, he stood, set his wood and knife down on the hearth beside him, squeezed her shoulder lightly, and then went out. A minute later she heard a door close and she looked questioningly to her mother.

"Evening chores." was her answer.

"Ahh." Ella nodded, though she had no idea what he could possibly do in the dark.

Eight

Ella sat on the wide bench behind the lawyer that had been assigned to her. A woman who had been assigned as her temporary guardian sat beside her on the hard bench.

Her mother and father—she was still working on getting used to the idea—sat on the bench behind them. She had turned to look at them several times, and when they sat down, she wondered why they didn't come up and sit with her. But when no one sat on the bench beside them, she figured there must be a reason.

One of their neighbors sat in a seat by the judge, looking more uncomfortable by the minute. The questions that were being asked were not precisely the sort of thing that were common knowledge.

Ella's situation was one of those things that most of their neighbors knew about. They had all seen her go back and forth running errands. But most of their neighbors were the type of people who didn't want to know what was really going on.

Ella had actually been surprised at how many of their neighbors were set to be in court. Of course, she also knew there was a possibility that the lawyers had done something to get the neighbors here. They had ways to do things like that... didn't they?

It was less than a minute before the judge dismissed her and called up the next person. Ella braced herself to listen to her whole life laid bare again.

I don't understand why they can't just take what one person says, and ask everyone else if that's how it was.

It was nearly painful, sitting here listening to it all. Somehow, it felt harder than actually living it.

The entire day had been a long line of all the people she'd had contact with over the last few years. The lawyers questioned maids, caterers, plumbers, carpenters, and a number of other people who had been hired to do things for Silvia at the house. They had brought up every single one of her teachers from school, the regular driver from the bus route she took, and the women who worked for the clothing designer Silvia typically commissioned to make dresses for Dorothea and Victoria. They had spoken to

Silvia's cook, driver, gardener, and even the person who did her manicures.

After several hours, they moved on to neighbors and even a few people from Silvia's social circles she could probably no longer consider friends—if their refusal to look in her direction was any indication.

At one point, the temporary guardian nudged Ella and whispered that she should sit up. She didn't realized that she had sunk lower and lower in her seat as people were questioned.

"Ella, you should not take any of this personally. It's not about you at all. It's about how you were treated." The whispered words were likely meant to make her feel better, but all they succeeded in doing was make her feel worse. As if it were not bad enough to have lived through all of this. Now she had to sit here and listen to it as the people of the jury sat there and looked at her as if she were the most pitiful person on the planet.

It would be enough to make anyone want to disappear.

* * *

To make matters worse, during the trial she was not allowed to stay with Silvia, but she was not allowed to stay with the Masts, either.

She was allowed to visit them for an hour each day, but every visit was also attended by her temporary guardian. Those times were filled with uncomfortable looks and long silences.

She had so many questions she wanted to ask, but she was almost afraid to. Watching her friends and neighbors being interrogated in court each day had given her the idea that there might actually be a very real danger she would ask something that might lead to something the guardian could possibly use against her family.

So, she made small talk as best she could,

which was beyond difficult since she knew so little about how her new family lived.

Fortunately, due to the ridiculous media coverage of the trial that would ultimately decide where she would spend the rest of her teen years, she was staying in a hotel near the court instead of a group or foster home.

She had been provided with a laptop to use and she spent hours on it, spending her evenings researching the Amish and their way of life—a life she hoped would soon be hers to live and embrace.

Reporters had rushed her every time she arrived for court. They all seemed to think the Amish people were backward and uneducated. She'd even gotten the impression that a lot of people thought she would be better off staying with Silvia and just putting up with her servant-like lifestyle.

But everything she learned about her birth parents' life made her wish the trial would move faster, and that she could spend her time with them.

She was excited to be part of a slower way of life, a place where family and community was central, in a home where she would be surrounded by love and faith and hope.

If only I could speed this trial up, and get the outcome I really want.

That was the only thing that really worried her. Silvia had a lot of money and a lot of connections all over the city.

Would blood... and truth win out over popularity or influence? Would she be allowed to return to the family she had lost before she was even old enough to know the difference? Or would she be forced to continue to live out the ridiculous fairytale gone wrong life she'd been dragged into?

Only time would tell.

Nine

Ella cringed at the headline that dominated the front page of the local paper for the city—a city that would shortly no longer be her home.

OUT OF THE FAIRY TALE AND INTO REALITY! Cinder-Ella is set to return to her simpler roots this week. Is life in the big city as 'the little cinder girl' more or less difficult than life on an Amish farm? Will trading in her broom for a bonnet be as easy as she thinks? Or will the harsh Amish life prove too much for the country girl who grew up in the big city?

Somehow, the combination of her name and the facts of how she had lived had come together to have everyone comparing her to her least favorite of all the fairy tale characters she'd read about.

Probably because I didn't want to see the parallels between her life and mine.

The thought left a bitter taste in her mouth.

Yes, she had been basically forced to work day and night in Silvia's house, caring for people who turned out not to be her family at all, but the newspaper—every newspaper—was making it sound like she might actually be working harder in Amish country on her family's farm.

For weeks, every newspaper and news

anchor who had mentioned the story had chosen to focus on the work aspect of her new life with an Amish family.

She dropped the paper on the desk in front of her with a huff. Did they really think so little of the Amish people? Had no one learned anything about how warm and welcoming and wonderful the plain folk were—or at least, had been to her so far, in the past weeks of a trial that had turned into national news.

They all wanted to report on the little cinder girl aspect. And everyone just assumed she would be cleaning the enormous farm, house and outbuildings all by herself. Or maybe they didn't care... they just wanted to make the story sound as sensational as possible to sell more newspapers.

She didn't see how her new life could possibly be more difficult than waiting on Silvia and her two daughters hand and foot, not to mention keeping their large manor spotless.

At least she would have help on the farm.

Of course, that was when doubt settled in. She should have help with the cleaning, but what if the rest of their way of life was too difficult for her? After all, they had no modern conveniences; no phones, no cars, no television, none of the things that most people took for granted in everyday life.

Not that I've had all that much experience with modern conveniences.

She thought sourly. About as convenient as her life got was an electric washer and dryer.

"Ella, are you ready to go and collect your things?" The social worker's voice interrupted her thoughts, for which she was grateful.

At least she could stop thinking such negative things. Modern conveniences or not, these people were her family, her real family. They truly seemed to love her, and they definitely wanted her. She'd done enough research to know that the Amish tended to stay far, far away from any sort of legal proceedings, so the fact that they had retained a lawyer, gotten involved in the legal proceedings, been present for every single day in court, and offered their lives up to the media and the public for all to see told her that they wanted her.

They had even rented a small house in the city so that they would be close by.

She couldn't imagine many normal people willingly going through the nightmare they had all just been through, much less a family that did everything they could to stay out of the spotlight.

But they had. And they'd done it for her, to get her back home, to get her out from under Silvia's thumb—and Ella knew, no matter what happened with her life there, nothing could be worse than what she had lived with for ten years at the hands of Silvia and her daughters.

Following Anne, the tiny woman, her

temporary guardian, who was only about an inch taller than her, felt weird. But Ella knew she needed the woman's help to collect her things. The court had ruled that Silvia and her daughters were not allowed within one hundred feet of Ella unless she were with an officer of the court.

Not that I have all that much to pick up.

The thought came as she got into the small car. She could only imagine what her cousins could have done to her room in her absence.

Mother's charm bracelet... John's books...

The man she'd always thought of as her father had imparted to her a love of reading. He'd been the type who never left the house without a book. And he'd spent most every evening by the fireplace, engrossed in a book. Many of those evenings, she'd been on his lap or at his feet as he read to her.

As she thought about the lovely books, panic rose up in her. Would she be made to toss away the books that were precious to her, or the charm bracelet; which was essentially the only thing she had left of the only mother she had known... up until two months ago anyway.

She had no idea what her new family, which was how she always seemed to think of them, felt about reading. Were there rules in an Amish home about books? Could she only read the Bible?

And she knew they didn't wear jewelry. Would she be allowed to keep the charm bracelet, if she never wore it? She ached at the very thought of losing the only things in the world that were actually of some value to her.

But, even as she worried, she knew it might be for nothing. If her cousins had gotten into her little room, they might have found her treasure box. If they had, they certainly would have the bracelet by now.

And the books... what would they have done with them? Nausea rose up in Ella's stomach and throat at the thought of someone destroying what little she could actually call her own.

Even though it was little more than a storage closet, it was hers and the thought of them destroying it... just because they could... made her want to be sick.

The feel of a hand on her shoulder pulled her from her worries. It didn't settle the sick feelings, but it did distract her enough that she reminded herself that there was no use getting all worked up until she knew one way or another.

"We're here, dear." Anne spoke softly, almost as if she could see the battle waging within Ella.

Then her hand moved as she got out of the car.

When Ella opened her door and stepped out, Anne was standing on the sidewalk, waiting for her and holding a large duffel bag that had laughter bubbling up unexpectedly in Ella, laughter that she did her best to choke back.

If Anne thought Ella owned enough to fill the large bag she held, she was in for a big surprise.

She must have mistaken Ella's lack of movement for hesitance. She reached out and patted Ella's shoulder. "It will all be just fine. You'll see."

Ella didn't bother to correct her. Nothing about the situation was going to be fine. Nevertheless, she followed, walking up the steps to a place she had never imagined leaving in such a way.

She had always felt certain Silvia would have asked her to leave eventually, but not for years, not while she was young and well able to clean up after her and her daughters, not when she had essentially free labor.

Her pittance of an allowance came from some sort of trust fund that had been left for her. She had heard her aunt discussing it on several occasions with the family lawyer. She was annoyed that she had to give any of it to Ella at all, determined that it should all be used to cover her care.

Ella coughed to cover the laugh that tried to escape at the thought. As if she had ever been on the receiving end of care from anyone in the past ten years. No, she had been the only one taking care of anyone there... everyone there.

She could only guess that the care she had spoken of was electricity, water, clothes, food, things like that. Though the scraps she managed to get hold of had barely lent themselves to what most would call a meal.

And the only clothes she had ever been allowed were castoffs, things that her cousins did not like and would not pass on to their friends, hopelessly ripped jeans and shirts that were stained or torn in ways that made them decidedly unfashionable. It made for a meager wardrobe and the more she thought about it, the more the thought of the plain dresses her new sisters wore appealed to her. At least they weren't ripped and stained, though they would likely be handed down to her from Aida or one of the older girls whose names she still couldn't seem to keep straight.

Silvia's driver answered the door, opening it with a frown that puckered his lips until he resembled some sort of hulking fish in a dark blue suit.

Anna went through her spiel about official business and fortunately, the man stepped aside and let them in, though he followed them up each flight of stairs, until Ella felt like she just might jump out of her skin. Did Silvia really think she needed to have Ella watched so closely?

If I were going to steal from her, I would have done it years ago. Disgust with the woman who was not actually her aunt made Ella want to turn and run back down the stairs and out the front door, leaving everything behind and hoping her new family would have mercy on her for showing up with absolutely nothing.

She kept going though, following the stairs up until she'd reached the tiny door that led to the only space in this enormous house she had called her own for the past ten years.

The door opened easily, but the mess that met them had Ella and Anna stopping at the threshold.

Dorothea and Victoria had definitely been in here. And there was the desire to run again. Did she really want anything they had touched... destroyed? Would there be anything worth salvaging in the disaster that stood before them?

She doubted it, but she moved across the threshold anyway, determined to discover the truth for herself.

She picked up a few things on her way across the room, but dropped each right back down again. Each piece of clothing had been practically shredded. Each of the few keepsakes she had collected over the years, mostly things she had from her first four years in the house, had been smashed or shattered.

She was quick to dash away the tears that escaped her eyes, determined not to give them any evidence that they had indeed gotten under her skin.

There was an odd sound behind them when she moved aside the loose portion of wall where she had hidden everything of real importance to her over the years.

She looked over her shoulder to see a look of shock on Silvia's bodyguard's face.

Good.

She smiled then. They hadn't found her hiding place. John's books and the charm bracelet would be safe.

At least I can leave here with something that is dear to me.

Ten

It was quite by accident that Ella overheard the conversation between Silvia and her lawyer. She had just finished packing away the last of her books, when she heard voices coming from somewhere. She only leaned forward to listen and try to discover where they were coming from.

She had never been one to eavesdrop.

She'd seen Dorothea and Victoria do it often enough—and heard them laughing over things they'd heard—to know that she did not approve of it. She also knew it would get her into an unimaginable amount of trouble with Silvia if she were to be caught at it.

The only thing that kept her where she was, once she realized she was overhearing someone's conversation, was her own name.

"The problem is that the will doesn't say daughter. It specifies Ella Wharton."

Silvia cut him off, her voice cold. "But that's not her name. That's not who she is. It shouldn't be legal"

"And I will argue that. I assure you." The lawyer spoke again, all but shouting at first. "All I am telling you is that it may do no good. The jury is not going to see it that way."

She cut him of again. "Then, they're wrong."

"They may be wrong, but Silvia, you have to realize how all of this looks." He paused a moment, as if he expected her to argue. When she didn't, he went on. "You knew what your sister had done, and even after she died, you told no one."

She broke in there. "And what exactly was I supposed to have done? It wasn't like I knew where she belonged."

"I know, and I will make that argument as well, I assure you. But we have been through one trial already, and it did not go well at all." He paused again before going on. "I fully intend to argue that you did what you thought was best, not having any idea how to return the girl or whether her parents might still even be looking for her. All I am saying is that you should prepare yourself for the possibility that you may lose everything."

"When she's of age." It wasn't a question. Silvia's voice was filled with authority and certainty.

"Not necessarily. They may elect to transfer the guardianship to her birth parents."

There was a loud bang, as if someone had dropped something heavy. "No. No. No! This cannot happen. I won't have it!"

Ella jumped back at the loud sound, and Anna turned to her. "What was that?"

When Ella looked to look at Anna, she panicked a little when she realized Silvia's driver was not there anymore.

Something deep within her, some voice deep in her thoughts whispered that she could be in trouble. Ella stopped transferring everything so carefully, positioning the bag so that she could just sweep the remainder of the books into it, turning to Anna just a moment later.

"Is there someone you can call?"

Anna looked perplexed. "Call? Who would I call? And why?"

Ella took a deep breath, trying to calm her speeding heart. "I don't know exactly. I just have a terrible feeling that we may not be able to leave as easily as I hoped."

A strange expression crept across Anna's face then. Not fear precisely, but something close. "Are you trying to tell me that they will not let us leave? That we could be in danger?"

Ella was already nodding. "Yes. That is exactly what I'm telling you." Panic had taken hold of her. She knew just how dirty some of Silvia's past dealings had been. The woman had no difficulty at all with intimidation or threats... or even blackmail, when it came to getting what she wanted.

"We'll just see about that." Anna pulled out her mobile phone, punched in a few buttons, and began to speak to someone.

Ella took the time to pack up the last few things from her hiding place, looking around the room one last time to see if there was anything else worth taking with her. When she spotted nothing, and Anna turned back to her with a sharp nod, she zipped up the bag and prepared to head for the door.

Anna put a restraining hand on her arm. "Let's just give them a minute, shall we? They're close, but..."

Ella nodded. Then, a minute later, when Anna nodded to her, she led the way out of her tiny room and made her way down each flight of stairs with Anna right behind her.

She had nearly convinced herself that they were in the clear when they reached the ground floor with no sign of Silvia or her hulking driver. However, Anna had no more than stepped off the bottom stair before Silvia, her driver, and the family lawyer appeared out of nowhere and blocked Ella's and Anna's path.

"Are you going already, Ella? Did you double check to make certain you packed absolutely everything of yours?" Silvia was being careful to keep her words soft, possibly in an attempt to make it sound as if she were only concerned, but Ella knew that tone; that overly cautious, icy cold tone that meant trouble was brewing.

Not to mention, Ella knew that Silvia knew very well what her daughters had done to the room and her things. She could even have been the one to suggest it to them. At least half the time, she was where they got their rotten ideas.

"I am going, yes. I packed everything worth taking with me." Ella was careful with her words too. She had learned long ago from the woman standing in front of her, how to say just the right thing; so that her words held an air of truth, but had an underlying bite that only the target would understand.

"You'll wait until the girls get home, of course. They'll want to say goodbye."

Ella quickly disguised her bark of laughter with a cough. There was no way Dorothea or Victoria had any interest in wishing her goodbye or good luck or anything else remotely positive.

They would only be concerned with who would be taking care of their every whim and desire now.

Fortunately, Anna stepped in then, saving Ella from having to make something up that sounded credible. She might be able to craft her words cleverly, but she had never been able to lie convincingly to Silvia.

"I'm afraid we must leave immediately. It is a long drive, you know." With that, she took Ella's arm and started around Silvia.

They'd taken no more than two steps forward before Silvia's driver blocked their way again—and Ella found herself gripping the bag she held a little tighter, shifting it a little in her grip. She might not be able to swing it hard, but she dearly hoped the weight of the books inside would be enough to do the job if she had to use it as a battering ram of sorts.

Fortunately, the doorbell rang just then, and the driver went to answer, Silvia right behind him. Anna let go of Ella's arm and took her hand, giving it a quick squeeze as she pulled her toward the door.

As they crossed the enormous foyer, Ella could see that there were two policemen in the opening, both with one hand on the gun in their belt, one of them with his foot wedged tightly up against the door itself.

Silvia and her lawyer were doing their best to convince the policemen that there was nothing to be concerned over and everything was perfectly normal.

The driver, who had been doing his best to shut the door, moved to the side as Anna came up beside Silvia, blocking their path again—and it was all Ella could do not to scream at the man, even though she knew it would do no good.

The policemen could clearly see her and Anna, and that Silvia's driver was blocking their way. One of them spoke up, loudly. "Sir, you need to step aside, now!" His voice carried quite a way and Ella could not help but wonder if he knew more about Silvia than she could guess. Nothing would make her obey quicker than having her standing in the neighborhood threatened.

Indeed, she hesitated for only a moment before turning to the massive man and telling him to let them pass.

Ella let out a very unsteady breath as Anna pulled her past a seething Silvia, her stony-faced driver and the sputtering lawyer.

Only when she was safely seated in Anna's small car and pulling away from the house that no longer felt like home, did she breath a little easier, though she found herself watching in the side mirror for any sign that Silvia's driver could be following them. Not that it really mattered one way or the other.

The Mast's address had been part of the court papers. If Silvia wanted to show up at their house, there was really nothing any of them could do to stop it.

Ella didn't really expect it though. Silvia

had everything she had ever wanted; the house, her sister's money, and no need to share one bit of it with anyone else. What reason would Silvia have for chasing after Ella?

Eleven

Ella was not prepared for her arrival at the Mast farm, though it became apparent quickly that her family had been preparing for some time.

It was nearly dinnertime when Anna pulled up in front of the house. Ella, looking around, wondered how long it would take before this place would begin to feel like home. Anna walked her up to the door, knocked, and waited for someone to answer.

Suddenly without any warning whatsoever, they were surrounded. Ella and Anna were immediately swept inside to a room packed so tightly with people, Ella was surprised there was room to breath, much less move.

While she caught—or tried to catch—her breath, she heard Anna speaking to her mother, who had opened the door. Ella couldn't hear anything that was said, but she was propelled forward through a crowd of people, most whom she did not recognize.

Beside her, Aida was talking nonstop, likely telling Ella who they were moving quickly past. But in her state of shock and the general noise level of the room itself, she heard not a word her sister said. She just nodded along, mumbled hellos, and shook hands with anyone who stuck a hand out as they passed by.

Questions rushed through her mind as they made their way quickly from one end of the house to the other. Would she be expected to remember all of the people she'd just been introduced to? Would she be seeing all of these people a lot? What exactly had her new family told them all about her?

Was no one shocked that she'd shown up wearing ripped jeans and a ragged tee shirt? Every other woman in the room was wearing a dress. Even Anna had on a skirt and suit jacket.

And just where was the rest of the family? Glancing over her shoulder, Ella caught sight of Jacob standing behind their mother, who was still talking with Anna. And Aida was right beside her. But where was everyone else in this crowd of strangers?

She wondered where Aida was taking her. They were still moving quickly, through the living room now. Aida pulled and Ella followed, but there was no clue to anything special in their path, just more people she didn't know.

Aida started up the staircase, motioning for Ella to follow her...

* * *

Ella bolted awake the next morning at her usual time. Across the room, Aida let out a loud gasp and sat back down on her bed with a shake of her head. Ella had the covers thrown back and her feet on the floor before she remembered where she was. When she did, she shook her head a little, trying to wake herself up.

"Ella, you don't have to get up now. *Mamm* said to let you sleep. I didn't mean to wake you. Why don't you go back to sleep."

"I always get up this early." She looked to where her sister was still sitting, a slightly odd expression on her features. Aida had obviously been trying to sneak out of the room without waking her.

"I startled you, didn't I?"

Aida shook her head. "No, of course not."

"No, I did. I can tell." She tried not to laugh, but the situation was almost ridiculously comical. Aida might say she wasn't startled, but her body language told a different story.

"Well, maybe a little." She stood then. "We just thought it might be nice for you to get some extra rest. That's all."

Ella smiled at the apology in Aida's voice. Her new family had sat through weeks and weeks of trial where neighbors and friends and business people she'd interacted with told the court about how hard she had worked every day for Silvia and her daughters.

They must think they were doing her a favor by not letting her help clean up after the party, or by letting her sleep in when everyone else got up to do their regular morning chores.

"A noble gesture to be sure." She shrugged a little before going on. "But since I'm up, I think I'll just come down with you, maybe help out with the morning chores."

To her credit, Aida didn't argue, but she looked like she wanted to. "Well, since you're up, you could *kumme* down, *jah. Mamm* and I would be glad of the company, for sure and for certain."

Ella stood, and went to the closet Aida had showed her last night. On one side there were what she'd called her *Englischer* clothes. On the other, there were dresses like Aida wore, eight of them, hung neatly in a row.

With another little shrug, she ran a hand over them. They were all such beautiful colors, it was difficult to decide which one she should pick.

When she sneaked a glance at Aida, she saw that her sister was wearing a dark blue dress that was almost black.

"I can see you are wondering if there is a *gut* reason I am wearing such a dark color this morning, *jah?*"

Ella nodded.

"Well, today is wash day. It can be a very dirty job." She wrinkled her nose a little. "The boys clearly have no idea just how dirty a job they give us."

Ella laughed with her sister as she pulled the darkest color dress out and walked back to her bed with a smile. She knew all too well how nasty a job dirty laundry could be, but she could not imagine how dirty clothing could get when a man spent all day out in the fields sweating. She wasn't entirely sure she wanted to.

But she did want to pull her weight. And if that meant dealing with nasty, dirty clothes, she would take it in stride. And she didn't see how it could possibly be much worse than some of the jobs Silvia had given her.

"I'm just going to duck into the bathroom." Aida said it as she slipped out of the room and gently pulled the door closed behind her.

Ella was grateful for her sister's gesture—and for the privacy, but still a bit thrown off by the general behavior of the entire family. They were all acting as if she were a visitor, which made sense in a weird way, but in another was really difficult to take.

She shrugged as she slipped into the dress that Aida had evidently made for her over the last few weeks. At least the newspaper had been wrong about life here being too difficult for her to handle. It was certainly an adjustment, but there had been nothing so far that she'd found she couldn't handle, only things that were difficult to believe.

The house had indoor plumbing and hot water, thanks to a gas water heater, which was a lot more comfort than she'd been expecting. They also had a gas range in the kitchen and a gas powered refrigerator. They had gas lamps in every room and, surprisingly, they seemed to give off about the same light as the fixtures she was used to.

When they had come up to bed the evening before, Aida had shown her the room they would be sharing, her new bed, and her closet. Then she had oohed and aahed over the books Ella hesitantly asked about.

Aida rushed off then, only to return a couple of minutes later with Jacob and one of their other brothers. They came into the bedroom, carrying a tall bookcase that they placed between the two windows on the far wall of the room, then hurriedly left, closing the door behind them.

After Aida helped unpack the rest of the books, she then carried them in small stacks from Ella's bed to the bookcase, where Ella lovingly placed them on the shelves.

When all of them had found a place, Ella emptied the bag of the few personal items that had survived the assault on her little room. Aida told Ella she could store the duffel bag either under her bed or in the top of the closet. Thankfully, she hadn't made a point of poking into the bag to be sure it was empty.

Just before Ella slipped it onto the narrow shelf in the top of the closet, she pulled the charm bracelet from the inside pocket where she had tucked it earlier that day. Then she slipped it into the small drawer in her bedside table, still wrapped in the handkerchief she used to try and keep it safe when she had tucked it away.

She simply wasn't ready to test her luck with a piece of jewelry, especially when it was something she held onto as a memory of the only mother she remembered.

They were good people, sure, but she wasn't sure they were that good.

Now, just as she placed the folded

nightdress on the narrow shelf in the closet where she'd found it the night before, Aida pushed open the door just a little, then all the way when she saw Ella was dressed.

When she picked up the kerchief to tie over her hair instead the *kapp she wondered at Aida's lack of comments, but again it was a pleasant surprise, so she kept quiet, too.*

In another minute, she was following Aida down the stairs, and then toward the kitchen. They didn't see anyone else up and about until they walked into the kitchen, where their mother stood at the counter, measuring out ingredients into a large bowl.

Aida breezed over to where she stood, singing out a *"Gut* morning." as she went.

Their mother returned the greeting. "And did you leave Emma sleeping upstairs?"

Aida was already shaking her head as Ella worked to remove the expression her face always seemed to twist into when someone called her Emma. Fortunately, she managed it before her mother turned around and saw her standing there.

"*Gut* morning to you as well, Emma." She paused a moment before going on. "You didn't need to get up. We agreed to let you sleep in, dear heart." Ella noticed a short hesitation before her mother said 'dear heart'. Either the expression had showed up again, or she'd done something else when her mother had called her Emma. Either way, she'd clearly noticed a reaction on Ella's part.

Determined to somehow get past it, she smiled and tried to infuse as much joy into her voice as possible. "Oh, I'm always up early. And I'm glad to help with whatever you need."

"*Ach.* You don't need to be working your very first morning here." She waved away Ella's offer with a smile. "But we would for sure be glad of your company."

Aida nodded her agreement as she moved

over to where their mother stood and wrapped her arms around her. They stood that way for a long moment before Aida stepped away and walked to the far end of the kitchen.

Ella moved closer to the counter, trying to decide if she should give their mother a hug as Aida had done, or not. Fortunately, the decision was made for her when her mother went right back to the bowl of ingredients in front of her.

And so, Ella stood, watching as Aida bustled around the kitchen and their mother measured ingredients, kneaded dough, and then as she placed three covered loaf pans into the pantry to rise while Aida pulled muffins from the oven, then prepared a chicken for cooking later in the day. They were such a wonderful team, chattering away as they worked, Ella began to wonder if she would ever fit in with them, or if she would just continue to be an outsider—only this time, it was in her own home, with her real family.

She was thrilled when Aida suggested she walk a bit, perhaps down to the creek. She even told Ella where she could find some berry bushes, making a fuss over how helpful it would be if Ella could do that, since they were hip deep in laundry by that point.

Twelve

 cooled by the thick, green grass. She watched the water rush past as a sigh escaped her.

"Is this seat taken?" The familiar voice shook her out of her reverie, and she started to scramble for her shoes. But, before she could find them, Chris had shed his as well, and was settling beside her.

They sat there together, in silence, for a long time as the river moved along its own merry little path, completely oblivious to anything other than the rocks and sticks in its path.

When Chris spoke again, his voice was low, smooth, cautious. "Is everything all right, Ella?"

"Do you know, you are the only one who calls me Ella without any trouble?" She knew it wasn't the answer he was after, but she honestly had no idea how to answer his question.

She could certainly laugh at the absurdity of it all. Everything should be all right. Everything should be perfect. She had the family she had always wished for, a home where she actually felt welcome, more than enough food with no guilt attached, and so far, only one chore to do.

She had nearly broken down and begged for something more to do that morning, but standing in the kitchen, watching her sister and mother do everything so easily, working together like a well-oiled machine, she'd been forced to admit that they really didn't need her help. She was certain Aida had only sent her after the berries as a way to give her something to do.

Eventually, they would have to give her more to do... right? If they didn't, she would be bored silly. She was used to being at the beck and call of three exceedingly needy people from the time she woke to the time she rushed off to school, and then again from the time she arrived home from school until late into the night.

But here... here she had exactly nothing to do so far, no more school to attend, and far too many options open to her to choose a proper leisure activity.

"So, you're not the only one having difficulty with the adjustment, then?" She looked up in surprise at his words. How did he know she was having trouble? Did she look as troubled on the outside as she felt on the inside? Was that what her mother had seen earlier that had put an odd look on her delicate features?

It must be because there was nothing else Ella could think of. They certainly weren't having any difficulty adjusting to the situation. Why in the world would any of them have any difficulty with the adjustment? They were going about life just like they always had. The only difference was another body in the house.

They hadn't given her anything to do except a mercy mission of sorts, and she was beginning to feel the boredom creep in.

To Chris, she nodded mutely, surprised at how well he had gauged the situation, and he didn't even live there.

"You just give them some time. They'll *kumme* around, and you'll be grateful later for the break that you're getting now.

She smiled at that. He had a point. If nothing else, she could look at this time as if it were a vacation.

"So, other than feeling slightly out of place, how are you adjusting?"

She laughed and nudged him with her shoulder. "It's only been a day. Didn't you just tell me to give it some time?"

"I did, yes." He laughed then, too. "I suppose I only wondered if everything is living up to your expectations or not."

Ella started to answer with another joke, but something about what he said made her stop. "What do you mean, exactly?"

"I mean, isn't this something you said you sort of dreamed about when you were a kid? Is it everything you were hoping for, after finding your real family?"

She thought about that for a minute. "Promise you won't laugh at me." She said it with no heat. She really didn't care whether he laughed or not. But he nodded solemnly and she started talking.

"For as long as I can remember, I've had two wishes, two fantasies in my head that I desperately wanted to come true." She paused for a moment when he nodded again. Clearly he was not surprised by her admission.

"The first, of course, is the obvious. I've dreamt all my life that my family would come for me. I never imagined all of this, mind you. I just always wished that some other relative who actually wanted me would show up and demand that my aunt allow me to go off and live with them."

He nodded again, not a hint of laughter in his expression, and she went on.

"I always felt like I would have to have some relatives who were better than the ones I was stuck with, and if they would just come to visit, they would see how much I needed to leave that house—and how much they wanted me with them... obviously."

"Of course." He nodded wisely.

She laughed a little at herself before going on. "Anyway, it was one of those things I fantasized about when I was younger. When I got older, the tone of the fantasy changed somewhat." Suddenly, she was all too aware of what she was about to say... to a boy... about her most romantic fantasy; and how he might take that revelation. So, instead of going on, she just shrugged.

After a very long, very full silence, he gently nudged her shoulder with his. "Go on. You were older and your fantasy changed."

She shrugged again before answering. "Oh, you know... I was growing up. I stopped wishing for such silly, childish things. That's all."

Somehow, he seemed to see right through her stumbling explanation... or perhaps he always had.

"So, your fantasy turned more toward what a young woman fancies?" He nudged her again as he said it.

She blushed. Heat rushed all the way from the tips of her ears to the middle of her chest, where her heartbeat sped up. Here she was, sitting all alone, essentially in the middle of nowhere. If the young man beside her had not been Amish, she might be worried.

As it were, she was certain she had nothing to worry about. He was Amish, and there was no way he would ever be interested in her. And if he were, he would have done something... said something... surely by now to tell her so.

Wouldn't he?

"So, are you going to tell me or do I have to guess?"

She looked up in surprise. Was he seriously expecting her to tell him about her silly, romantic, girlish, fairytale fantasy?

One look at his face told her that he was.

"Oh, you don't want to hear about it. It's so silly." She waved a hand dismissively, suddenly desperate, if it were possible, to keep from having to voice what felt unexpectedly personal all of a sudden.

"I do want to hear it, actually. But, if you don't want to tell it..." He trailed off, leaving her an opening big enough to drive a truck through.

It was easy to see he was not going to let go of it until he heard the whole story so, still blushing, she started again. "It feels so silly when I think of it now, but I always enjoyed fairy tales. I mean, I really, truly enjoyed them. I loved everything about every single one of them, and I used to fantasize that I would have my very own *happily ever after* someday."

When he said nothing, only smiled, she pushed on. "I always wanted the whole sappy, romantic scene. You know what I mean, the handsome prince rides up on his white horse and rescues the girl from her terrible step-family."

When she finished, she looked down at the water again, and it was some time before he said anything. When he did, it was even better than the most perfect response she could have hoped for.

"Being plain doesn't mean you can't have a fairy tale. It just means it won't be fancy."

She laughed then. He was absolutely right about that. There was nothing fancy about her family or his. They were certainly about as plain as you could get.

The question was, would that be enough for her? Could it be enough? And...

How would she ever know whether it was enough if she didn't try?

Thirteen

The next morning, while she and Aida happened to be outside hanging the wash, a very official looking car came down the long driveway.

When Ella first spotted it, she nearly panicked, worrying that Silvia had somehow found a way to get her back, to take her away from the place she was finally beginning to feel she might call home some day.

Aida didn't see the car at first. Facing Ella, she had no way to see it coming. Only when it got close enough to hear the crunch of tires on gravel, did Aida turn around to look.

"Hmm. Wonder what that could be about." Aida spoke softly, almost under her breath.

Or else, the pounding of my heart is somehow clocking out normal sound.

Ella forced herself to take deep, slow breaths and focus on the pins she held in one hand, the dress she held in the other.

By the time she had gotten it onto the line, her mother had come out the front door, watching the car as well.

Ella nearly called out to her, begging her to go back inside, thinking maybe if they all ignored the car, it would go away.

But she didn't call out and the car kept coming. Aida even turned toward the house to watch their progress on the surprisingly smooth gravel drive.

When the car parked, two men and one woman got out, all three in suits.

Is this good news or bad?

Ella had no way of knowing, but there was a churning deep within her that told her at least some part of it would be bad news.

The trio walked up to the porch, spoke to her mother intently for several minutes before one of them broke away and headed toward the side yard where Ella and Aida were hanging the wash.

The woman looked from one sister to the other and back again before calling out.

"Which one of you is Ella Wharton?"

Aida answered before Ella could.

"Actually, her name is Emma Mast."

That stopped the woman. She stood looking at the two of them, confusion obvious in her expression. Then she looked down at the papers in her hand—at which point, Ella decided to speak up.

"It's me you're looking for." The woman looked up at her, then back down to the papers in her hand. Ella went on. "She's right. Technically speaking, my name is Emma Mast, but I'm certain your papers say Ella Wharton. That's what Susannah Wharton, the woman who abducted me, named me."

Ella shook her head a little before continuing. "She even fixed it somehow. I have a birth certificate, a social security card, and an old passport with that name."

"So, you are Ella Wharton, then?" The woman still sounded very confused as Ella continued to move forward, so she nodded. If this was going to be bad news, she really much preferred getting it over with.

"I am, yes."

The woman looked over Ella's shoulder toward where Aida still stood for several seconds before turning her attention back to Ella.

"Is there somewhere we could speak in private?"

Ella looked toward the porch where her mother stood, her hands clenched tightly together, her face a tight mask of worry. What had those two men said to her to have her so freaked? Whatever it was, it couldn't have been good.

"When you say private, would that mean you don't want anyone else with me?"

The woman looked at her with a very strange expression. She shook her head a little as she leaned back in surprise. "No, I suppose you can have anyone you want with you."

"All right then." Ella turned toward the house, not even watching to see if the woman followed. "We can talk inside."

When she stepped up on the porch, her mother reached out to her. Ella hesitated only a moment before taking the offered hand. If this was the last day she could spend with them for awhile or if something else had happened, she would certainly not deny her mother that tiny comfort.

Her mother led them all into the house, and then into the living room. She offered everyone refreshments and the men took her up on her offer. The woman did not.

Ella stood when they sat, facing them and watching as her mother walked out of the room.

As soon as her mother was out of earshot, one of the men spoke up. "Miss Wharton, I'm certain you're wondering why we are here."

Ella wanted to argue, to ask him to wait, to tell him she didn't really want to know, but she knew they were going to say whatever they had come to say one way or another, so she figured the easiest thing would be to just let them get on with it.

She nodded.

"We are here to fulfill your mother's last wishes, to carry out the terms set forth in her last will and testament."

Ella looked toward the door that led to the kitchen, where her mother had just disappeared, momentarily confused.

Then, just as the realization dawned that he was speaking of Susannah Wharton, the woman who had abducted her, the man said her name, confirming her thoughts.

"Mrs. Wharton left her entire estate to you, Miss. It has been held in trust until you come of age." When he stopped and looked over to his companions, Ella took the chance to jump in.

"I'm sorry. What?" And then, before anyone could answer, she added, "And also, I'm not of age yet."

The same man spoke again. "We are aware of that, Miss. However, due to recent discoveries that have been made along the lines of your true parentage, the court decided to award you special dispensation, given your current circumstances."

"My current circumstances? Special dispensation?" Ella repeated the words, but was not entirely certain she understood what they were telling her.

She had been prepared for them to tell her there had been some sort of mistake... that Silvia had found some loophole to drag her back to the city and servitude, not to find out that she was receiving something from the estate she'd been certain she would never see a penny from.

"Yes, Miss. Your formal legal guardian, Silvia Stockton, was given control over Mrs. Wharton's estate immediately following her death."

Ella nodded slowly, and he went on.

"This was to be the arrangement until your twenty-first birthday, when the entire estate would be transferred into your possession."

His words were beginning to make sense, but they were no less frightening.

"With the outcome of this most recent legal battle, and the truth about your true parentage, and the aforementioned having previous knowledge of your kidnapping and having made no effort to return you to your rightful family, the jury chose to award you the full estate immediately and in full."

With that, he pulled several thick bundles of papers out of a thick folder he'd been holding all the time. "You will need a parent's signature, as well. However, with you being only months from your eighteenth birthday, it was decided this would be the simplest solution for all parties involved."

Ella looked up at the gasp. Her mother was just inside the doorway, holding a large tray filled with thick slices of the bread she and Aida had made that morning, several glasses, and a pitcher of lemonade.

She rushed to take the tray before her mother dropped it, worrying the whole time. How much of the conversation had she just heard? What was she thinking about whatever she had heard?

And then there was the question of what

all of this meant for her? If she chose to become Amish, would she have to give up the estate? Did she even want it?

She had no answers, even though she knew there were more questions to be asked. So she busied herself with the tray, setting it down and pouring lemonade for the trio who had shown up and essentially thrown a wrench into her otherwise normal morning.

"You're not taking her away." Her mother spoke suddenly, forcefully, surprising Ella. "She belongs here, with her family, her real family." She moved over to stand right beside Ella, putting an arm around her and pulling her close.

The man in front of them looked at Ella, then back to her mother, then back to Ella, who only shook her head.

"Mom, they're not here to take me away."

Ruth gasped again from beside her, but didn't step away. "Then, why..." She trailed off as she gestured to the papers he still held out toward Ella.

"They brought papers for me to sign... about my... about the estate that apparently was left to me by..." She trailed off then, unsure of what to call the woman who had taken her from her true family and then left her in the care of someone who had essentially mistreated her for years.

The man spoke up then, still holding the papers out. "These papers are only the documents needed to legally transfer Mrs. Wharton's estate from Silvia Stockton to Miss Ella Wharton."

Ella nearly winced at the name. Her family was still having a lot of difficulty with calling her anything other than Emma. It was getting easier for her to remember that she was who they wanted when they said that name, but when he said it, so matter-of-fact like that, it was as if she had never been anyone else and never would.

"Will it actually make a difference that my name really isn't Ella Wharton?" She didn't look at her mother, but she did feel her stiffen a little beside her.

The man cleared his throat before answering. "Actually, as far as the government is concerned, your legal name is Ella Wharton. You can always petition to have it changed, but unfortunately, and for the immediate future, you will be known that way by everyone... except perhaps the people here." He added the last almost as an afterthought, looking toward her mother, but not directly at her as he spoke.

Ella nodded her head again. She probably should have been relieved. She'd been trying to figure out exactly what everyone was supposed to call her, to figure out if she was really Emma or Ella or what, and here he was telling her that she was legally the name she knew herself as best.

So, why didn't she feel any better? Knowing that her mother was standing right beside her, listening to this man talk about money and a name that had been given to her by the woman who took her away from them could not be easy.

But she didn't argue. She didn't put up a fight. She just stood there with her arm around Ella, her hand squeezing gently.

After what felt like a very long time of staring at the sheaf of papers in the man's hand, Ella squared her shoulders, cleared her throat, and spoke.

"What exactly do I have to do?"

Fourteen

Sitting in the large barn, on a blanket that was draped over a bale of hay, watching the little groups of teens chatting, Ella thought back to sitting in front of the computer screen at the public library.

She'd read everything the internet could find about how the Amish—or *plain folk*, as they preferred to be called—lived, worked and played. Some of it had sounded far too good to be true. But far more of it had sounded too absurd to be possible.

There were things that she simply could not believe about the wonderful people she had met so far, things that must be made up for the sake of entertainment or by someone determined to smear the good name of these plain people.

Yes, they were people. Therefore, they were imperfect. But she refused to believe that anything about their way of life was meant to be intentionally cruel or vicious. They were good people. Of that she was certain.

Everything she had seen... every one she had met so far... had been warm, welcoming, and kind to her. She only hoped she could find her place among them.

When Aida had suggested she come to the singing this evening, Ella's first inclination had been to politely refuse. She'd read about their singings, the community gatherings where the youth of the district got together to sing and socialize, but she had no real reason to be there. She had not even decided whether or not she would become a member of the community, and dating was supposed to be a big part of these sort of events.

Then there was the fact that the only people she knew here were family, and she couldn't even remember all of their names yet. Meeting more new people was not precisely at the top of her list of things to do.

And then there was the fact that she had never been very good in social situations with other teens. For years she had longed to be included, but when the time had finally come, it had been a disaster from start to finish.

She was nothing like other teens. She would rather curl up with a good book than be in the middle of a crowd of people. She would rather be alone at a table in a coffee shop than at a party. And she would rather spend her time learning than flirting.

English or Amish, she had a feeling that she would never truly fit in, and she'd been telling herself for days that finding her true family was enough for her.

Then Aida had rushed in, talking about a singing and how she just had to go with her and meet all the other youth from the community. Ella had not had the heart to tell her sister that it would be a bad idea.

Everywhere she looked there were groups of teens clustered together and chatting. Some of the groups were quite large. Some of them were only two people... or four, clearly made up of couples.

Watching the mating ritual that didn't seem all that different on the surface from the parties Victoria and Dorothea had always teased her about, Ella could easily admit she preferred this to the wild parties they went on about all the time.

There was no music blasting loudly, so

that you couldn't possibly hear anyone without being up against one another. There were clearly no cliques. The only person not involved in a group was her—and that was entirely by choice... her own.

There was also none of the fashion competition that had only served to give Ella a headache when she'd been listening to stories from the girls. At least half of their conversation had focused on who wore what, who had been a fashion train wreck, and what the new styles were for that week.

Ella had never understood how something as simple as clothing and shoes could cause such distress, competition and jealousy in teens, especially teen girls.

Of course, some of that could have been due to my having no fashionable clothes to speak of.

She let out a contented little sigh at the thought of her closet at home. Not only did she have quite a few new things, they were all hers and no one was going to purposely destroy anything just because they could.

It was a breath of fresh air. That was for sure.

When one of the smaller groups drifted closer to her, Ella debated with herself for nearly a minute before giving in and slipping away. She scooted off the hay bale and made her way quickly and quietly to the large open doors, then out and into the night, moving around the doors to where she would be out of sight.

Once outside, the sky captured her attention completely. Everywhere she looked, there were stars. She could not remember a time she had seen so many, except in pictures.

Logically, she knew it had to do with being away from the lights of the city, but the fanciful part of her mind felt like it was something more, something special about being out here in the country, surrounded by God's people.

Perhaps they are a little bit closer to Heaven.

The thought made her smile. She certainly felt that way herself, as if she had been lifted up to Heaven these last few days. Her only complaint was that she did not have enough to do—and deep down she knew that was a really silly thing to complain about.

"Beautiful, isn't it?" The voice came out of the darkness from beside her. Ella jumped and tensed her muscles to run before she remembered where she was.

This was not the city, where she had to be careful not to be anywhere alone after dark. This was the country—Amish country —and she was safe.

"Forgive me. I didn't mean to startle you." With those words, she recognized the voice, though she still couldn't see Chris in the dark.

"It's all right. No harm done." She answered, laughing a little at herself for being so easily frightened.

I thought I was tougher than this.

A moment later, she added, "It really is a beautiful night."

He made some noise she took as agreement, but said nothing—and, after several long seconds, she went on.

"You would never see these stars in the city."

"*Jah.* There's too much light." His answer surprised her. She wanted to ask him if he knew from experience, but the words stuck in her throat. Especially after what he had said to her down at the creek about a fairy tale, she felt unexpectedly nervous.

How had he known what she had been thinking? And how had he said almost exactly what she had just been thinking?

Before she could think about it more, he spoke up again. "Do you miss it?"

His words took her by surprise, and she wasn't entirely certain what he meant. "You mean the city?"

"Jah. The city... and your old life?"

She started to answer with a negative, but before the words were out, she realized she did miss it, a lot more than she had expected to... or at least, she missed parts of it. Yes, she had wished for a different life, but she had never really envisioned it being this different.

So she nodded as she answered. "A little maybe, though I really don't know why." Then she shrugged. It was the truth—and she wondered how she could ever miss something that had mostly made her miserable.

She looked back up at the sky, but no answers winked back at her from the stars above.

"I understand. I missed home when we moved here, even though things there were not at all *gut* for some time before we left. It's an odd feeling, *jah?"*

She nodded again before remembering to answer out loud too. "Yes, it is."

They stood there in silence for a long time, looking up at the sky and listening to the sounds of the teens in the barn behind them. And Ella started to wonder why Chris was standing outside the barn, with only her for company. Surely such a handsome young man had a girlfriend somewhere in there...

It was several minutes before she got up the nerve to ask. Then, just as she opened her mouth to voice the question, he spoke.

"Ella, there is something you should know." There was something about the sound of his voice that told her this was not a good thing. She braced herself for bad news.

"I am not particularly proud of this, and I do not know how you will feel about it all, but I think it only right to tell you before I... well, before..." He trailed off and she took a deep breath, bracing for what was sounding worse and worse by the second.

"When my family moved here five years

ago and I met your sister, I felt an attraction for her. I have done everything possible to make her aware of those feelings." He turned then, taking a small step until he stood in front of her. She looked up at him, curiosity at war with concern. Had she done something she shouldn't by sitting at the river with him with her shoes off? She certainly didn't want to come between her new sister and her boyfriend.

Did I do or say something tonight to cause a problem?

She wanted to ask him, but waited as he went on.

"It has never been more than that, I assure you."

Ella opened her mouth, but closed it before saying anything, confused by his words.

"I do not believe she has returned my feelings one bit, and looking back at the time we have spent together, I must admit that my attraction to her was no more than that." He took her hands in his then, holding hers gently as he brought their joined hands to his chest. "I believe that attraction was perhaps *Gotte's* way of giving me a reason to befriend your family."

He stopped for a moment and Ella looked up at him, the confusion building within her, compounded by the strange flickers of fire that licked over her skin at the touch of his thumbs as they stroked lightly over the backs of her hands. She tried to think of something to say... anything... but nothing made sense in her head.

"I now see that the only feelings I have for your sister are brotherly... friendly, which is only fitting since I have every intention of courting her sister."

He brought one of her hands to his lips then, gently brushing his lips across her knuckles. The same fire spread from where his lips touched her skin, making every thought in her head turn to mush.

"Ella?" He said her name in a low voice, barely disturbing the haze that had filled her head. When she said nothing, he repeated himself a moment later, a bit louder and in a voice that that sounded more confused than it had been a moment before. "Ella?"

The confusion got through to her. That, and the fact that he stepped back a little, his body heat disappearing when he did. The sudden rush of cool air against her over-heated face managed to clear some of the fog in her brain.

"I'm sorry. I must admit, I feel like I've missed something here."

He started to step closer again and Ella reluctantly pulled one of her hands from his grip, pushing against his chest a little. His being so close was doing something strange to her and she wanted the chance to think clearly for a minute. She would never figure out what was going on if she didn't.

"I am sorry, Ella. You don't feel the same way." He started to pull away, but she was already shaking her head.

"No, that's not it at all."

He moved forward again with a smile on his face that told her he had plans to kiss more than her hand, but she pushed against his chest again.

"No, wait. Please."

He stopped moving forward. There was confusion on his face, but fortunately no anger. He only nodded.

She took several deep breaths while she tried to make sense of all the thoughts swirling around in her head. There was so much she wanted to say, so much she needed to know, as well as much she was afraid to say or know. She had no idea where to start with it all. And, even though he had stayed where he was, he had not dropped her other hand. The heat that had started where his thumb had rubbed was spreading, carrying confusion along with it, threatening to make mush of her thoughts again.

But she didn't want him to let go.

"This is too much for you right now, *jah?*" He spoke softly, but with a certainty she didn't feel.

She wanted to tell him no, but knew she would be lying if she did. She didn't want to lie to him.

His hand cupped her chin gently, lifting her chin a little until she was looking at his face. After a moment he nodded, as if he had seen his answer in her face. *"Jah,* it is too much now."

When she started to drop her chin, he held firm. "Ella, listen to me, please." She looked back up and he went on. "Your life has been difficult for a very long time. In the past few months, you have had some very difficult things to deal with. Your entire life has been changed." He was nodding again. "This is not something you must deal with right now. I have waited this long. I can give you the time you need."

The breath she hadn't realized she was holding came out in a little explosion of air and he laughed. "I am not at all certain how to take that, but I will hope it is only relief that you have time to think things over."

Ella nodded and smiled. "It is, really. That's all it is. I promise."

"I suppose this means you will not want me to shine a light in your window tonight, then." While she tried to figure out what that meant, he went on. "May I at least take you home?" She nodded as he stepped back, pulling her with him as he turned to go back inside.

Her moment of panic had turned back to confusion. There were so many things about their conversation that she had thought meant something they might not.

I will have to ask Aida what all of this means.

Suddenly, she was in a rush to get back home. She had a lot of questions for her sister.

A moment later, looking up at the man beside her who still had hold of her hand, she admitted that she was not in that much of a hurry.

When they walked back into the barn, he steered her toward the tables where all sorts of refreshments were set up, only letting go of her hand to put a plate in it.

Fifteen

Ella sat on Aida's bed shaking her head. "Wow. Okay. I had that whole conversation wrong."

A moment later she swatted playfully at her sister's shoulder. Aida had started laughing, and she was so loud, Ella was certain she would wake the entire house. "Stop that. It isn't that funny."

"It is if you think about it." She shook her head a little, but thankfully, stopped laughing. "Poor Chris. All those years he was wanting to court, and I had no idea how to tell him I did not return his feelings."

Ella still wasn't certain how she felt about that little tidbit. Even though Aida had explained that courting was what they called dating, and Chris had assured her they never had, it was more than a little odd to think that he could have been here dating her sister... if Aida had let him.

But why does that matter when I'm not even sure I want to date him?

The question was one she didn't have an answer for. She had never been in this sort of situation before. No boy had ever shown this sort of interest in her... or at least, none that she'd noticed.

Not that you've let yourself notice.

The memory of how tightly Silvia had watched her... not to mention the crazy amount of things she'd had to do in a day, had never allowed her much time to pay attention to boys.

"Do you like Chris?" Ella looked up at Aida's question. Her voice was filled with an enthusiasm that reminded Ella of listening to Dorothea and Victoria when they were excited about something.

Is this what is it to have a sister to share things with?

The thought sent a warmth through Ella, along with an emotion she was completely unfamiliar with.

She felt... a welcome, she felt as she were at home, like she had finally found her place in the world.

* * *

It was the giggling that woke Ella later that night.

She sat up and looked around the room, wondering if Aida was giggling in her sleep.

The sight that met her searching gaze told her Aida was not sleeping.

She was rushing past Ella's bed, fully dressed, with her shoes in her hand, and a hand over her mouth.

"Aida, where are you going? Is something wrong?" Ella spoke quietly, somehow feeling like it would be a bad idea to wake anyone up.

Aida gasped quietly behind her hand and Ella almost giggled at the comical expression on her sister's face as she turned.

"Ella, I didn't mean to wake you." She stood there, clearly at a loss for words, her shoes still dangling from her fingers as she looked everywhere but at Ella.

When she turned to look at the window, Ella remembered what she had read about in her research at the library about how the Amish teens dated.

Without really meaning to, she giggled. Poor Aida looked so comical. Ella debated internally for a minute about whether she should let her sister off the hook or pretend that she didn't know what was going on.

Would Aida forgive her for delaying her date?

Not willing to take the chance, Ella laughed a little, then sat up and spoke quietly. "It's okay, Aida. I know what's going on. I read about it at the library. Go. Have fun."

Aida's face lit up with her smile and she nodded, moving past Ella's bad and out of the room in her stocking feet.

Ella strained, listening for Aida, but no sounds reached her ears and after several minutes, she decided Aida must have made it downstairs and outside.

She smiled, thinking about Aida making her way outside very carefully to meet a boy that no one knew she liked. It was terribly romantic.

When she'd read about it at the library in the city, she had thought it must be terribly risky to go out alone, late at night with a boy. But after spending some time with the people in the community, she realized there was less risk in how they went about it than there would ever be outside the Amish community.

If I had given Chris any sort of hope, it could have been him at the window for me.

The disappointment she felt confused her. Why should she feel sad to know that Chris was giving her the time she had said she needed?

With a deep sigh, she started to slide back under the covers, but something caught her attention. There was a light outside. She watched, waited, and saw it again. It was a thin beam of light bouncing over the ceiling above the window.

Had Aida forgotten something? Was she feeling guilty about leaving her new sister behind? Was something wrong?

With that in mind, Ella climbed out of bed and headed for the window, a gasp escaping her lips when she saw Chris in the yard below.

"Ella, quick. Get dressed." Aida's voice sounded from behind her and Ella whirled. "Let's go. I'll show you where all of the noisy spots are." Her grin was wide and nearly lit up her face.

Ella debated for less than a second before turning to wave down at Chris, hoping he understood that she meant just a minute. Then she was heading for the closet. She hesitated a moment when it came to grabbing clothes. Should she dress Amish for something like this.

From the door, Aida's voice sounded again. "Just grab anything, Ella. Chris has seen you both ways."

Ella nodded, grabbing the jeans and tee she was more comfortable in and pulling them on quickly in the dark. How had Aida known exactly what she'd been thinking?

Could that be a twin thing?

She wondered while she dressed, but had

no answer. They had been separated for fourteen years, and she had never felt any sort of mystical bond to her long lost sister in that time.

Had Aida? She had no answer.

But then, she knew about me.

Whether she'd remembered having a sister or not, the family must have talked about her. Had Aida ever felt some sort of tenuous connection to Ella? It was a question for the next day, not when the boy she might like was waiting downstairs for her.

When she was dressed, she grabbed up her shoes and followed Aida out of the room and down the hall, careful to step where she did, and avoid spots on the floor that Aida pointed out.

They made it down the stairs with no noise, to Ella's surprise, and Aida led her to the side door, which was open partway.

A boy she recognized, but whose name she did not remember, was standing just outside with his flashlight pointed down at the porch.

"Chris, they're here." His voice made Ella wince. Didn't he think he was maybe being a little too loud?

"Tom, shh. The door is still open." Aida whispered from in front of her with a little laugh.

When they got to the door, Aida slipped through quickly, turning sideways and being careful not to push against it. Ella imitated her, certain her sister was showing her the door would be too loud if they opened it any further.

The boy she had called Tom was holding the door in place, likely in case one of them brushed against it accidentally. She moved past him and then sidestepped Aida as her sister turned back to close the door slowly.

Then she followed Aida down the short flight of stairs and across the lawn. Chris met her halfway, his arms out in a gesture that she couldn't quite identify.

Once she was right in front of him, he finally spoke, his voice barely loud enough for her to hear, definitely not loud enough for anyone else to hear.

"I took a chance." When she nodded, he went on. "I figure, this is how we do things." He shrugged, but went on before she could say anything. "You can't make a decision about whether you want to adopt our way of life unless you experience it all, right?"

She nodded, suddenly unsure. Was he doing this because he really liked her or because he was trying to be a good neighbor or something?

"Plus, I wanted to see you again." He reached out and took her hand and her breath hitched at the strange feeling that rushed through her from the contact.

She nodded again, but he said nothing else. When he turned away from the house and started walking, she moved with him.

He led her across the gravel drive and

around the corner of the barn, where a small buggy waited. He helped her up into it first, his hands lingering only a second or two on her waist while he helped her settle into the seat.

Then he was moving around the front and climbing into his own seat. "You ready?"

She could only nod again as they set off.

Chris got the team going slowly, but he didn't move around to the front of the barn. Instead, he turned them in the opposite direction and headed off down what was little more than a path through the grass.

The buggy traveled away from the house, the barn, the other outbuildings, and across the fields. Chris concentrated on the horses, and Ella sat beside him, trying to figure out what to say. What did one say on a late night outing with a young Amish man?

She almost wished that Aida were there to give her some pointers, but Aida and Tom had either gone off in another direction or they were too far ahead or behind to be seen by Ella's hesitant glances.

She sat beside Chris, looking up at the stars and watching the fields go by, and waited for him to say something.

It was several minutes before the fields gave way to grass, and then for a narrow gravel connection to the main road to appear. When Chris turned onto the road, Ella thought she saw another buggy ahead of them, but she couldn't be sure so she didn't say anything. They followed the road for a long time until Chris finally spoke up.

"I meant what I said earlier. I'm happy to give you time if that is what you need, but I enjoy being with you, so I hope you'll let me spend time with you as often as possible."

When she looked up at him, he smiled. "I will not push you to decide anything, and we do not have to court... what you would call dating, I believe." She nodded and he kept going.

"I enjoy spending time with you. I will take whatever I can get." That, coupled with his warm smile sent strange little shivers up and down her spine and a warmth spread across her middle, filling her with such a wonderful feeling about the whole situation, that she didn't think anything about what she was doing.

She leaned into him, slipping a hand under his arm and laying her head against his upper arm.

After a moment, he turned to her, still smiling, even though there was quite an intense expression in his eyes, and then he was pulling the buggy off the road into an open area where there were several other buggies parked around a large bonfire.

There were two couples outside of their buggies, standing close to the fire. Three of the teens looked as if they were roasting marshmallows or hot dogs, she couldn't tell which. While the fourth was simply standing beside the young woman he was with, one arm around her as she slowly turned the long stick she held out over the flames.

Chris stopped the buggy about the same distance away from the bonfire as the others who were already there, turning to her with that same smile and serious eyes.

"Does that mean you want me to court you, then? Have you decided to stay with us?"

And Ella knew the answer, realized she had always known it. There was so much emotion in her throat though, she could only nod.

His smile widened. His hands took hold of hers. And then, he was leaning toward her. He moved slowly, giving her plenty of time to move away or put a hand up to stop him, but she did neither of those things.

She sat there, waiting, watching his face as he got closer. Then, just before his lips touched hers, he reached up to put a hand on her face. Her eyes fluttered closed with the hesitant pressure of his lips on hers.

That same fire that had spread from his

touch earlier was there on her lips now. It warmed her all the way to her heart, as did the way his hand rested on her face, his thumb brushing ever so slightly against her cheek as he kissed her.

He had tilted his head just a bit as he moved toward her, and now his lips moved over hers a little as one thumb caressed her face and the other rubbed gently over the back of her hand.

The fire spread to her face, then raced across her chest while more rushed away from her hand, up her arm, and met the fire in her chest, filling her entire body with warmth and a strange sort of fluttering.

With a little sigh, she leaned closer to him, and he continued to kiss her, sliding his hand into her unbound hair. Sometime later, he scooted just a little closer on the bench they both sat on, then he let go of her hand to slide his other hand into her hair as well.

She had no idea how long they had been

kissing when he gently eased away, but she felt as if she were in the midst of a fog. Her thoughts were unsteady. Her vision blurred at the edges. Her mouth felt warm and soft and slightly tingly from his kiss.

When he spoke, his voice was deep and husky, his words quiet, with a hint of what sounded almost like frustration to her. "As glad as I am you're going to stay, I do have to admit I like being able to get at your hair this way."

She felt a blush spread across her cheeks. There was something about the way he said it that made her feel almost as if he were suggesting that there was something sexy about her hair, about being able to run his hands through it, which he was still doing.

And then he was kissing her again and she stopped thinking about her hair or anything else.

Epilogue

The next morning was a first for Ella. She woke with a light heart, a song on her lips, and a wide smile. Across the room, Aida was humming a little to herself as she sat up, then she smiled and stretched slowly.

"Well, I certainly feel more at home now." Ella spoke softly, still uncertain how much she should say where there was a chance of anyone hearing her. From the research she'd done, she knew teens usually kept these things to themselves until they were ready to declare their intentions and, while she secretly hoped Chris was feeling like she was today, she knew better than to wish for the moon.

Only once in her entire life had she ever wished for something and, so far, this was so much better... so much more... than what she'd wished for. Not only did she have a family of her own now, but she had a twin sister who she already loved, and she was courting a very special, young man.

Never would she have imagined that her life could ever be so blessed.

Turn the page

for exclusive

Bonus content

DISCUSSION QUESTIONS

1) It is very sad to hear that a child has been abducted, yet it happens... we read about it in the news all the time,, although most people don't really think it could happen to them. How did you feel when the Mast's little girl was stolen from her family? Do you think the Mast family should have kept their children away from the road—and the fruit stand? What would you have done if you had been there?

2) Chris was shocked to see his friend at the mall after she told him her family needed her help and she couldn't go. And she was dressed like an Englischer! Was he right to believe she had lied to him? Would you have doubted her, too? What do you think Chris should have done? What would be the best way to handle such a situation?

3) Once Chris talks to his friend Jacob, he discovers another identity for the young girl he ran into at the mall. Do you think they did the right thing by going back to the mall right away to see if they could find her? Do you think Jacob should have told his parents first?

4) Inviting Ella to have coffee at the mall seemed like the best way to have a chat—and get to know her. After all, she didn't know either of the young men and she most likely would have felt uncomfortable if they had suggested doing something else. Do you think it was a safe choice to make? What would you have suggested?

5) After chatting with Chris and Jacob, Ella learns what happened to Jacob's younger sister when she was three years

old. Knowing how unreasonable her aunt could be, do you think she made a mistake, taking Chris and Jacob home with her? How did Ella expect her aunt to react? What should she have done? Would you have done things differently?

6) After Ella comes home with the news that Jacob believes she is his sister, her aunt refuses to allow her to leave the house for several weeks. Finally, she sneaks away to the mall, only to run into Jacob and his sister—her twin sister. She agrees to go with them to her parents' house, where she meets her whole family. Can you imagine, after never receiving any love and support from the family you grew up with, the excitement of meeting a family you had only dreamed of, but never expected to have?

7) Thankfully, after going to court, Ella is allowed to live with her real family. Although she is eager to help out at home, her family do their best to encourage her to rest. During the court hearing, they learned about how Ella had always been treated like a servant to her aunt and cousins, not just because she was forced to do all the work and run all the errands, but physically and emotionally treated not as part of the family, but as their servant. Would you have stayed as sweet and cheerful as Ella? If not, what would you have done?

ABOUT THE AUTHORS

Naomi Miller mixes up a batch of intrigue, sprinkled with Amish, Mennonite, and English characters, adding a pinch of mystery, and a dash of romance!

Naomi's days are spent focusing on her writing, editing and homeschooling her grandchildren. She loves her career as an author, blogger and inspirational speaker.

She schedules several book events each year and enjoys the opportunity to meet readers face-to-face. When she's not rushing to meet a deadline, Naomi loves to make time to attend writing conferences, workshops, and other author events.

Whenever time permits, Naomi can be found in one of two favorite places. . . the beach and the mountains. . . usually with a book in her hand.

Naomi loves traveling with her family, singing inspirational/gospel music, taking daily walks, and witnessing to others of the amazing grace of Jesus Christ.

Ruth Miller writes sweet Amish romances filled with faith, fun and forgiveness. Her interest in the Amish began with her name. She went in search of plain roots and was dismayed to discover there were none. Still, she travels to Amish country at least once each year for research and fellowship purposes. *And for fun as well.*

Ruth holds the plain people in the highest regard and believes they provide us with an example of the sort of Christ followers we should all aspire to be. In the high tech world we live in, we may not all be able to *"go Amish"*, but that is no reason we cannot incorporate some of their principles into our everyday life. Simplicity, living with less. Appreciating nature, forgiving others more readily, and trusting in God are values that can only make our lives better.

When Ruth isn't writing, swimming or reading, she is bragging to her friends about her precious babies. Family comes first with Ruth and she cannot get enough time with hers.

ABOUT THE PUBLISHER

Christian Publishing for HIS GLORY

S&G Publishing offers books with messages that honor Jesus Christ to the world! S&G works with Christian authors to bring you the best in "inspirational" fiction and non-fiction.

S&G is proud to publish a variety of Christian fiction genres:

inspirational romance

young reader

young adult

speculative

historical

suspense

Check out our website at

sgpublish.com

DON'T MISS BOOK TWO

An Amish Fairy Tale

HER Beastly Blessing

NAOMI
MILLER

RUTH
MILLER

BOOKS BY NAOMI

Blueberry Cupcake Mystery
Christmas Cookie Mystery
Lemon Tart Mystery
Pumpkin Pie Mystery
Chocolate Truffle Mystery
Peach Cobbler Mystery

A Mother for Leah
A Suitor for Rebekah

Sophie Finds a Family
Sophie Celebrates Thanksgiving
Sophie's New Home

COMING SOON

AMISH SWEET SHOP ROMANCE
FROM INTERNATIONAL BESTSELLING AUTHOR
NAOMI MILLER
coffee
BEAN
connection